Laura was from a small town where she grew up with a big family and life was simple. She had moved to New York City and secured a job as a marketing executive which she absolutely loved. But after she married Edward, who was an only child from a wealthy family, she started to realize that money was not everything and Edward was not someone who was capable of love. It seemed that he changed after his father's murder which was never solved. Laura was thirty six and longed for a baby but Edward did not share the same ideas. He was in love with himself and his money but not Laura.

Laura left for California and while she tried to figure out what to do next and relaxed at the beach house, her creativity started to bubble to the surface. As she worked with her new ideas, she met the guy next door one morning after her run on the beach. His name was Kevin Khris and he seemed so perfect. Things got heated between the two of them. He made her feel things that she had never felt with anyone but she knew it was all just physical.

After Laura was informed that Edward's mistress, Brandi was twenty two, she did not take it well. He had bought Brandi a penthouse and deposited a couple million dollars into an account opened for her. Kevin was her sounding board when all of it went down. And as Laura appreciated his companionship and shoulder to cry on, she assured him that the relationship they had was never going to become anything especially when she found out how old he really was.

But when she ends up running into Joe Venetti, a lost love from her past, while on her way to join a hiking group, things get complicated. She felt that he had been her soul mate before Edward but they were young and things just fell apart without knowing what actually happened. Seeing each other opened a door that had not been closed after all and they picked up from where they left off or so she thought.

As Joe and Laura start to bond and spend more time together, Kevin finds out and he is less than happy for her. So, as the love triangle pursues, things really start to turn and the triangle is the last thing that anyone has on their mind. Everyone is fighting a secret that no one EVER knew existed except for Edward.

As the secrets of Edward's family become clearer to Laura and a big piece of the past comes to light, things become more dangerous for everyone around her and there is no place to hide.

From the author of Paradise Valley, Lost and

Found

JODI VILLONE

DANGEROUS GAME OF BETRAYAL

Dedicated to those in my life who have been so

supportive:

Family, friends and my wonderful

readers/followers

Thank you

Cover Design by

SelfPubBookCovers.com/Shardel

CHAPTER ONE

"I just don't understand why you don't want to have sex with your wife" Laura screamed at Edward and she slammed the door behind her. She had tried going into the bedroom he had started sleeping in, for God knows why, when she awoke this morning to see if she could give him a little wake up of her own. He had refused her loving touch which set her off.

Her heart was ready to jump out of her chest and she could feel the blood burning through her veins. Her fists were so tight, she realized that she had dug her nails into her flesh. "Well, I'm fucking awake now" she said aloud as she made her way back into her bedroom. She heard him walk downstairs and decided to pursue the conversation.

"Talk to me Edward. What the hell is going on?" Not only did she feel neglected as a lover, but also embarrassed that he refused his own wife and was also sleeping in another room.

He turned to Laura and the look that he gave her was of nothing she had seen from him before. It was freakish and cold and so intense she wished she had not followed him down. He started slowly coming towards her and she was so terrified, her muscles froze. He was standing an inch away looking down at her and almost in a growling tone said, "I told you. I've been extremely busy and am under a lot of pressure and you are adding more stress by creating a problem that is all in your head. Maybe you should be speaking to a shrink." And he turned back around and headed to his office.

Laura stood there shaking. She didn't know if it was from fear or from anger. Maybe both. She was too shocked by the whole incident to even know how to react to it. She slowly sauntered back upstairs to get herself ready for the day but the one thing she couldn't seem to shake was the look in Edward's eyes. Never in the five years that she had been with him had she seen him act like that. *Maybe he is just really stressed and it IS all in my head.*

Thirty six year old, Laura Jennings, sat at her desk, wondering how she had gotten where she was today. She had a successful career as a marketing executive within a big company. She loved what she did even though it could sometimes be very demanding. She was a stunning woman with wide brown eyes and long lashes. She had full lips and dark brown hair that she kept long and perfectly groomed. Her breasts were full against her thin body. She was very strong and confident and knew what she wanted in life.

Laura and her husband, Edward, were always working. He was an executive and an investor so any extra time he would have for Laura after work was used up while in his home office. It seemed as if lately she was non-existent. She had needs too. She never understood how such a young, powerful man would so seldom want some kind of sexual release. She was starting to think it was her.

Edward was thirty six as well and very handsome. He had come from money and learned very young how to take money and make even more. He too had dark brown hair but he had beautiful green eyes. His father was very powerful but he was never close to his parents, especially his father. His father had been murdered a year after they were married which was about three years ago and after that, his mother ended up losing her mind, or so Edward claimed, and is now living in a mental hospital heavily sedated. He would never allow Laura to visit her and she never knew why. It was a mystery and so secretive that she knew not to ask any questions. And as their marriage went on, Edward was starting to show his dark side. She felt that it might have something to do with the police never able to solve the crime. Maybe he was worried that he might be next but he did start to become a little more paranoid as time passed. The killers left the scene squeaky clean and took off with millions of dollars' worth of jewelry and found the money in their study. Edward's mom, Elizabeth said they had taken around two hundred thousand dollars which Edward could not understand why they would have that kind of money in their home.

Laura on the other hand worked for everything, even at a young age. She grew up in a household where her parents struggled at times. Her mother was an at home mom raising her and her four siblings. She was the second eldest. Her father worked as a contractor so when the economy was slow, the work was slow. But somehow, they always managed to get through. That's what made her into the strong and independent woman she was today. She still appreciated all the little things in life and their family couldn't be closer.

Laura wanted to start trying for a baby. She and Edward had had this conversation many times before as they had been married for four years now. But Edward was adamant that kids were not in his future. She wished she would've known this BEFORE they had gotten married. Laura thought she would be able to break him down eventually and even figured as he aged, he would start thinking children as well but that theory was showing to be seriously incorrect. So, as she was packing up her things in her office to go home, she figured she would try to have this conversation one more time. Maybe a baby would help their marriage....bring them closer together.

She knew Edward would not be at their home at this hour so she grabbed herself a salad on the way. Their house was in a very prominent neighborhood in New York. It was very big and very beautiful. Her home was classic and simple and way too quiet for Laura. She didn't feel as if it was home to her. It was definitely missing something. She missed her days of the past. The chaos at home and helping out around the house. Here, there is nothing to come home to. Not even a husband.

As she thought about her friends that she seldom speaks with, she set up her laptop in the living room. Her friends were a huge part of her and she felt like it was a sacrifice that she made marrying Edward and moving out to the city which she was starting to regret. But she loved her job and she wouldn't give that up but if she hadn't been so damn good at what she did, Adam wouldn't have found her eight years ago and she would have been content with her old employer by her family and friends and never would have met Edward. Adam came across her work and sought her out to give her an opportunity to work on something that would use her talent to the fullest. He offered to contract her out on some accounts he had that were distinguished and famous throughout the United States. One contract paid her more than a year's salary so she couldn't say no and she was able to travel back and forth to work on the projects from home and meet with Adam once every week at the office until they were complete. It was perfect. The best of both worlds. And then she met Edward.

She started thinking about her greatest love lost, Joe Vinetti. He was, she felt, her soul mate. Laura wasn't sure what or how it happened but them splitting up was a huge mistake. It left a void in her heart. But it was so long ago, it was just a fading memory.

As she waited for Edward to come home, she started searching online for a possible vacation for the both of them since she had not seen too much of him lately. Maybe that was what they needed. They seemed like they were drifting even farther apart lately. She was yearning for some kind of bonding. She then heard the door and the alarm. She heard Edward shut off the alarm and put his keys down on the entryway table. Laura stood up and walked in to greet him with a smile, "Hi, honey, how was your day?"

"It was busy but okay" he said as he walked past her too occupied to give her a kiss.

"Edward? I was thinking about taking a vacation with you soon. We have both been so busy and you have been a little stressed and we haven't had sex in a while" and she smiled trying to make it less serious.

"Laura, I don't have any time to take. Possibly, in a few months' time".

Laura feeling like she was slapped in the face added, "I would really like to make love with you tonight".

He looked at her and maybe it was the look on her face but he actually walked over to her and gave her a hug and kissed her on top of the head and said, "Let me get some work done first. Give me a couple of hours, you know I'm really busy" and he walked in to his office.

Laura stood there and started to feel angry and really upset at the same time. *How can he treat me like this?* she thought to herself. She tried not to cry but tears were welling up in her eyes. "That's it!" she yelled and stormed into his office. He was looking at a file and was starting to dial the office phone. She startled him and he quickly hung up the receiver.

"What is the problem Laura?"

"The problem is Edward that we have not had sex in three months. Why is that? What is going on that you are too busy to have intimate relations with your wife?" He looked at her and rubbed his face.

"Listen, Laura. You knew I was a busy man before you married me."

She interrupted, "Not this busy. You don't even acknowledge you have a wife. It's been four years and I want a baby. I'm sick of the excuses. Do you want a divorce?"

"No, of course not. Divorce is for quitters and Us Jennings do not get divorced. It would be a disgrace to our family."

"What family Edward? There is no family left. Who would it be a disgrace to?"

He didn't know how to respond, "Well, I can't have the papers getting a hold of that."

"Edward, I don't care. If you don't love me any longer, than we shouldn't be married. And seriously, you make it very hard for me to love you. We don't even sleep in the same room anymore."

"I've already told you it's because I work so late and I don't want to wake you up when I come to bed."

"I think that is a whole lot of crap." And she walked out of his office and went upstairs and cried herself to sleep.

Edward never came to bed. She thought MAYBE he would come in to apologize. He always slept in the guest bedroom. He even moved some of his clothing over there. This had just slowly started happening within the last six months or so. When she got up the next morning, she found Edward was already gone. *Did he even stay here to sleep?* She thought to herself. She decided to take a look in the guest bedroom to see if the sheets were slept on. *Huh. Did he even go to sleep last night?* It hadn't looked like anyone had been in there or showered even.

She went downstairs, checked the office just in case, started the coffee and came back up to prepare herself for the work day. *Maybe I'll go on vacation myself so I can think this through.* As she grabbed her computer and coffee, she headed out the door. On the way she decided to call her mom to see if she could drive out there for a long weekend. They lived in upstate New York in the same place she grew up. It was about six and a half hours from NYC. Her mom must have seen the caller ID, "Good morning Laura".

"Hi mom. I was wondering if I could visit you and dad for a few days. I need to get away".

"Laura, you know you are always welcome. Is something wrong?"

"Besides my marriage falling apart? No. My job is great."

Her mom sighed, she knew that Laura had been wanting a baby and was not happy at all with who she married but as a mother, she didn't want to interfere. "Come on out and we'll have the family over and you'll forget all about it."

When Laura got into work, she went into Adam's office. "Good morning" he said with a smile.

"I started work on the Fine design account" she stated.

"Okay. Do you need anything from me regarding that account?"

"No, Adam but I do want to see if I can take off early Friday to head out to my parent's house."

"I don't see a problem. You know you don't have to ask me. You're my number one here and you can take off whenever you want. You work all the time and you never take time so take it."

Laura blew out a breath of air.

"Sit down, Laura." And he pointed to the chair. "Is everything alright?"

She looked at him in thought and said, "I'm not sure. Things with Edward are not going so well. I mentioned divorce but he freaked out and said that divorce would ruin the Jennings name. I just need time with my family and friends."

Adam smiled, "Of course. I don't like Edward anyhow. You know how I feel on the whole subject."

Laura stood up, "Yes, I do know." And she smiled and said, "Thanks" and walked to her office.

She packed her bags when she got home. She got to work early so she could leave early. She actually left at ten so that she could make it to her parents by early evening. The drive was very uneventful. She planned on not only seeing her family but getting in touch with all her friends that were still in the area. She still saw her girlfriend Jessica who had two kids, Caleb and baby Callie. She spoke to her quite often and saw her whenever she was in town which was not very often. This would be good. She could catch up, relax and work at the same time. When she pulled into the driveway, it was a comfortable relief that came over Laura. "Home sweet home", she said to herself as she smiled and grabbed her bags.

She walked in the door and smelled home cooking. It was around six thirty and her mom had dinner waiting for her. "Mom?"

Her mom, Grace came around the corner, "Oh Hi sweetheart" and gave her a big hug. "How was your drive? I have dinner waiting for you in the kitchen."

Laura smiled, "My drive was good and I smell it. Smells delicious and I'm starving."

Grace grabbed her hand, "Come on and sit. I'll grab you a plate."

"Where's dad?"

"Oh he's sitting in the living room reading."
And then she yelled in, "Tony, Laura's here."

As Laura enjoyed her parents company, she ate every bite of her dinner. Of course her dad wanted to know more of what was going on with her.

"So, your mom said you and Edward are having some marital problems."

Laura looked at her mom, "Really? You didn't need to say anything to dad."

Grace cleaning up the kitchen said, "Oh, Laura, you know we are worried about you."

Tony sipped his coffee, "You are too smart and beautiful for that guy. He doesn't give our family the time of day. Out of the four years you have been married, we have seen him once. I don't like that. Why couldn't you have found someone who appreciated you more and treated you better and actually came with you to family functions?"

"Dad, I am fine. We'll figure it out and yes, I know. Edward wasn't the right one. How was I supposed to know that when I married him? He was kind of normal then."

Grace interrupted, "Why don't we change the subject. This isn't what Laura came out to visit us for. I'll pour us some wine and I can talk to you about the get together tomorrow."

"Mom, it's just going to be family right? I just want to relax and visit with my brothers and sisters. Nothing crazy. And I'm going to see Jessica tomorrow morning."

"Oh that's fine. They're not coming until early afternoon. Everyone is bringing a dish to pass."

As her mom went on about things that were rather uninteresting, Laura started drifting off and thinking about other things. About how much fun she used to have here with her friends and how less complicated life seemed to be. And she started thinking about Joe wondering how he was doing. After eight years, she still remembers how great they were together.

When she awoke the next morning, she quickly dressed and got ready to head over to Jessica's. She was hoping she could get some feedback from her about her problems with Edward. After all, friends are looking at everything from the outside in and have a better intuition and advice than family.

As she held Callie and watched Caleb play, Jessica knew a little of what was happening in Laura's life and couldn't believe that Edward went from charming to a total jerk. But again, just like Laura's family, Edward spent very little time with any of her friends.

Jessica knelt down in front of the couch where Laura was sitting with Callie. "So, when are you having a baby of your own?"

Laura looked sadly at Jessica, "We just had a discussion about this which turned into a fight a couple nights ago. He made it very clear that he does not want children now or in the future."

"What? Are you kidding? Laura that is grounds for divorce. What and the hell is his problem?" Jessica was furious.

"That's kind of why I'm here this weekend. I asked him for a divorce but he said that it would be a disgrace to the Jennings name and he didn't want it all over the papers."

Jessica glared in thought, "You need to get a good lawyer. If he is unwilling to be a husband whether it be in the bedroom or having a baby or even being supportive at all, then you need a to get out of the marriage so that you can start fresh. Who in the hell does he think he is?"

Laura shook her head, "He's a powerful and wealthy man who feels that he is entitled to whatever he wants and asks for."

"Well, I'm sorry Laura, he's being a selfish asshole and needs a kick in the balls."

That made Laura smile.

After a couple of hours at Jessica's, Laura didn't know if she felt better or worse about her situation but she knew what she had to do next.

After a weekend of being with her parents and catching up with family and friends, it was time to head back home to once again, confront Edward. He never even called her the entire time she was gone which she thought was a little strange but she knew things were falling apart. It didn't make it any easier. She left on Sunday morning and ended up getting home around three thirty in the afternoon. Edward was not there which she didn't understand so she gave him a call on his cell phone and got his voicemail. She didn't leave a message. She got settled in and was ready to go back to the office in the morning.

After a very long day at the office, she finally packed up to head home. When she got there, she decided to have a glass of wine so she went to the wine cellar to grab a bottle. She opened it up and poured herself a big glass and opened up her computer to start comparing some of her work with other accounts to see what she could add or do to make this Fine Design account pop. As she was working and starting to feel more relaxed she heard Edward come in. It was now eight thirty. Laura didn't even get up to greet him. She was too upset. When he walked past the family room, she spoke up, "It's pretty late for just getting home from work. Where have you been?"

She heard him sigh, "I had a late meeting and then we decided to get dinner out."

She turned to look at him. "Who did you have dinner out with?"

"Really Laura? Are you trying to accuse me of something? I was out with Bernie, Charles, Tom, Sherry ad Tonya."

Laura sat there for a minute, "okay, I guess I'll make something here. I thought we would go out for dinner together for once." He just left and walked into his office. And that just made Laura's blood boil. *He was very defensive over a simple question?*

Laura gave him a few minutes to settle in and she also needed her heart rate to slow down before she went in there. *I have to confront him. I need more than this.* So, she walked to his door, knocked and opened. "I know you are lying Edward. I can't live like this anymore. It's not fair to me. What is going on? I need to know. You never even called me to see where I was this weekend. For all you know, I could've ended up dead and tossed in the woods or were you even here at all this weekend?" Edward sighed.

"Why don't you sit down a minute? I have something to tell you". As Laura came into his office, she started to feel nauseous.

She sat down, "okay, I'm listening".

He looked at her and saw the intensity in her eyes. "I'm not sure if there is an easy way to discuss this but now that you mention divorce, I think it might be the right thing to do. We both have different visions and I don't want to stop you from being happy."

Laura looked at him in disbelief. "You sit here and talk about divorce with no remorse or any inkling of apology. Like it is a freaking game to you. I want the truth. Gloves are off. Are you fucking someone else?" He flinched as she said it as he never thought she would even consider it.

There was silence for a moment and then he answered, "Yes". Laura's anger felt like it was going to explode. She was normally a very sensible person but this put her over the edge.

And she screamed, "You asshole!!! You are a piece of shit! I don't care who she is, I am taking you down. You have ruined the last five years of my life. I've never hated anyone………………ever. But you Edward are one hated man right now. Good thing I'm smarter than you are. I have so much money saved, the lawyer I'll be able to retain will bring you the pain". Edward didn't know what to say. He knew he was wrong and knew she had sources. Laura got up and stormed out of his office slamming the door behind her. This had been building up inside her for a while.

She went upstairs to her room and cried. She cried so hard her head hurt and her eyes burned but she eventually cried herself to sleep with the tissue box next to her.

She awoke in the morning and the first thing on her mind was what an unfeeling asshole Edward was. She wanted to hit him so hard last night. She was proud of herself for keeping it together. *I will get him back but I will do it the right way……..hit the bank accounts.* She was good about saving and investing. It was all in her name too. Edward made enough and had enough that she banked her money and he paid for everything. *Thank God*, she thought to herself. She got up and looked at her puffy red eyes in the mirror. She grabbed herself a shower and got ready to go in to speak to the boss man. Adam was a great boss. Not only was he very hard working he was also dedicated to his wife and kids. His career was extremely important but he always made his family his first priority. He was empathetic to people's issues but knew when to let them know enough was enough. But she was pretty much partner in that company she worked so hard and was the best at what she did. She grabbed her laptop, keys and purse and headed out to her car.

As she walked into the office, Adam saw her and waved her in. She started to tear up but kept it in check. She didn't want everyone to know her business. "What in the hell happened? You look shot."

She ran her fingers through her hair and said, "Thanks. It was a rough night."

Adam looked at her with curiosity, "Did something happen?"

"Yeah, I'm getting divorced."

"Well that's great news. I've never been fond of Edward anyhow. There was always something about him that I could never pinpoint."

Laura shook her head, "There is a lot to it that led up to this."

"Laura, I've known you for what? Eight years? I know you. And I know that Edward was not the right guy for you the day you married him. So, what happened last night?"

She sighed, "First of all, I have asked him on several occasions about having a baby. He shot that idea down every time we discussed it but you kind of know that. And the past year, he has been so busy that he comes home from work around seven thirty sometimes later just to lock himself in his home office and work in there until all hours of the morning. So, it's not like we have had intimate times lately. He doesn't even sleep in our bedroom anymore. So, I asked him about a vacation. That we needed some time away. And he told me he was too busy and just walked into his office. I stormed in there and asked him why we hadn't had sex in three months. He told me he was cheating on me and wanted a divorce. Like it was no big deal. He wasn't even remorseful. We have spent four years….well five of our life together and I never knew he couldn't feel any love. I'm not sure now that he ever loved me. He is such a bastard." She wiped away the tears that wet her face.

Adam shook his head, "God, what an asshole. Listen. You are still working on the Fine Design account. You need to get away from here. You work all the time. You are here all the time. You have no life. I don't need you here. Here are the keys to my vacation home in California. I know you have seen pictures so you know that it will be very relaxing. Just work on the account from there and keep me in the loop. If you need more time, let me know. I will contact an attorney friend of mine that deals with divorce matters. I'm sure he will get you more monetarily than you got emotionally in the five years of your life you wasted on that piece of crap." Adam came over and gave her a huge hug.

She backed away and looked at him, "Adam, thank you so much for understanding. And not just that, for being a good friend to me. Gloria is very lucky to have a husband like you. I'll call you when I get there."

"Okay kiddo. Remember..........You're still my number one here and all my top accounts go to you and I need you at your best so whatever you need, let me know."

"Thanks Adam."

CHAPTER TWO

Adam was not only her boss but he and his wife Gloria were absolutely wonderful to her. Adam was forty seven and Gloria was forty five. They had three kids. Devon, who was ten, Maria, who was eight and Tessa, who was six. They were adorable. And because Adam was so dedicated to both his work and family, Laura spent a lot of time over there going over work related issues. As Laura sped home to get her bags ready, she called her mom, Grace to let her know what was going on. "Mom, I just wanted you to know that I'm fine. That I am now going through a divorce."

"What? How did this happen?" Grace asked.

"Edward told me he is cheating on me and he wants a divorce."

"Oh my God!" was all Grace could say. And then she ranted and raved while the only thing Laura could do was listen. "Well that no good cheating bastard. Who does he think he is? Your father is going to go nuts. He was worried when you married him that he would do something like this. Not trustworthy, he said."

"Mom, please…….I'll be okay. He didn't want kids anyways and I do. So, it will all work out. I'm a little upset that I was betrayed and basically lied to for five years but now I'm free and the healing can begin."

"Oh honey, come back here and stay with us. You can go to the lake and relax up there."

"Actually mom, my boss gave me the keys to his vacation home on the coast of California so I won't see you until I get back………..okay? Give me a couple of weeks. He told me to work from there and to try and get rest. He is contacting one of his lawyer friends and hopefully, we can get this divorce finalized quickly."

Her mom sighed, "I'm sorry that you have to go through this. It's not fair."

"Mom, I am strong and can get through this. You and dad never cared for Edward anyway. I will call you when I get to California. Love you."

Just then, she pulled into the driveway. The first things she did was go online to find a flight. Then she grabbed a cup of tea and started up the stairs. She pulled her luggage out and started packing. As she did, she started to feel a pit in her stomach. She felt as if she failed at something so important. "I hate him", she said out loud. "I hate him for making me feel like the failure." Just then, she got a weird feeling to go into his office to look around. He had been acting so strange lately, she wanted to see if there was something else going on besides having a mistress.

As she slowly took a look around his office, she pulled out drawers and turned on his computer. Just wanted to find something that popped out at her. *Who is this girl?* She wondered. *And does this girl know he is married? Does she know about me? Has she been in this house?* Then she found a deposit slip of some sort. She found it stashed in the back of Edward's planner. It was a deposit of one million dollars into an account to a Brandi Stevens. Her name was Brandi Stevens. *Brandi Stevens?* "Who is that?" she said aloud. And she also started searching in drawers and in the back of one of them pulled out a piece of paper that had several online transactions dated ten, eleven and twelve years ago for a guy named David but no last name. She didn't think much of it. It might be an investor with Edward or maybe it was from his dad. She grabbed the one with Brandi's name on it and headed upstairs. She had to get finished packing. Her plane left at one o'clock and it was already eleven.

She wasn't even going to leave a note or let Edward know where she was going. *Let him sweat it out. Thinking I could be home any moment. What an ass* Laura thought to herself. She grabbed her bags and loaded them into her car and ran back in to get the rest. As she was on her way to the airport, she didn't know what she was going to do with her life now. Where was she going to live? She knew she didn't want the house. It never felt like a home to her. She was going to start fresh. Laura was going to find a home that fit her personality and was a part of her.

She checked her bags and waited in line for security. For a Tuesday, it was pretty busy. She thought she would maybe give her friend Jessica a call once she got to Adam's Cali house. She had seen pictures of it many times and it is beautiful. She was invited many times but Edward was always too busy to go with, so she always declined. The three story house sat on oceanfront property with glass windows all the way around for a panoramic view. You had a view of the ocean from all sides. It was an amazing home. Adam's father had bought just the land and then gave it to Adam in which Adam and Gloria then built their dream home. They even joke that it's much nicer than their permanent residence which is much more meager.

She boarded the plane and actually fell asleep for a little while. She was so exhausted from the previous night. *At least I'll be able to run along the beach in the mornings*, she thought with a smile. She knew she would have to rent a car which she had done online and probably stop at a grocery store to get some food. As she waited for her bags to come around, she checked her phone for texts and calls. She grabbed her bags and got on the bus to get her rental.

When she finally finished her journey and made it to her destination, she was actually still pretty tired. She made herself some tea and sat on the deck overlooking the ocean. *I could so live here all year round*, she thought to herself. *I'll get to work tomorrow*. She called Adam to let him know that she was there and everything was great.

"Laura, please try and relax. I left a message with my friend, Jack Larson, the attorney and I'm waiting for him to call me back. In the meantime, just work from there and if you need anything, just call me."

"Adam? Thank you. This is breathtaking. You are a great boss and even better friend. You and Gloria are part of my family. I will call you tomorrow after I do some more work on my account."

Laura decided to take a walk on the beach and she called her friend Jessica while she enjoyed the sun and the sand. "Don't worry Jessica. I'll be okay. I'm a big girl. How is my little guy?"

Jessica responded, "Caleb is doing wonderful. And baby Callie is so sweet. I can't wait for you to see us again. I wish I could fly out there to be with you. I'm worried. I hated that guy. Didn't I warn you about him? Damn it!"

"Jessica, I know. Everyone warned me but myself. I think deep down I knew something wasn't right but I also knew that I had taken myself out of the dating world and was exclusive and didn't necessarily want to start it all over again. He was sweet when we were dating. But if I had known that he would never want kids, well, that certainly would have broken it off."

Jessica sighed, "Well, now you need to get this finalized and move on. You still have it going on. You are so beautiful and successful and have a great personality. You kind of lost a bit of yourself being with that jerk but now you can get back your old self again. Call me in a couple of days so I know you are okay. I'm just a phone call away."

"Thanks Jessica. I know. Miss you guys."

After they hung up, Laura was amused at what Jessica had said. She hadn't really thought that she lost herself being with Edward but now that Jessica mentioned it, she saw it a little clearer. "It's time to get me back", she whispered to herself. As she walked, she caught a glance of a very handsome gentleman that looked to live next door. He seemed to be about thirty five, with blond hair, blue eyes and a body that anyone would say yes to. She didn't want to show any kind of desperation so she just waved and kept on walking. But he watched her. He watched her walk all the way to the beach house.

She grabbed a sandwich, a glass of iced tea and her laptop and again, sat out on the deck. She wanted to at least check her emails and then thought about the deposit slips she found. "I need to put a face with the name." She ran in and grabbed it out of her purse. She typed in the name to do a search but there were so many Brandi Stevens that any of them could have been her. "It's probably the little stripper right there. Or that little blonde bimbo. Oh it doesn't matter. It couldn't be an investor because that would've been recorded with his company and not just on a deposit slip laying around. It does matter that he deposited that much money into an account for her. That much the attorney will know."

She watched the beach walkers while she ate and relaxed. The breeze was like the wind was whispering to her. It calmed her soul. And then the phone started ringing, she looked and it was her older brother, Dominic. "I'm not even answering it" she said to herself. And then she thought, *Great my whole family is going to be blowing up my phone.* She knew they were just upset and wanted to let her know they were behind her in all of this and she was sure they had been keeping their thoughts to themselves for some time about Edward and couldn't wait to let her know what they thought of him.   As she was in deep thought about all of that, she heard someone yelling up to her from the beach.

"Hey, can I come up?"

"Sure", Laura responded. *Oh my gosh………..it's the guy from next door*, she thought. When he came up he introduced himself as Kevin Khris.

"Well, Hi. I'm Laura. She didn't know if she should give out her married or maiden name which was Brooks.

He looked at her with his dazzling blue eyes, "Can I sit?"

"Oh, yes, please. I'm sorry" Laura said. "Would you like a drink?"

"Oh no thank you. I just wanted to come over and introduce myself. I usually see Adam, Gloria and the kids over here but then I caught a glimpse of you."

"Yes, Adam and Gloria are friends of mine and Adam is my boss as well. I'm just here on a working vacation for a while. I needed to get out of the city for a while. Well, Adam kind of pushed me out and made me take the time off. Long story I wish not to get into."

Kevin smiled at her, "Okay, I won't pry. I will however, ask if you would like to go to dinner with me tomorrow evening."

"Oh, that is so very nice of you Kevin but I'm not sure I feel like being out in a crowd yet", Laura said apologetically.

"No, No that is fine. Could I interest you into coming over to my place so that I could cook you dinner?"

Laura smiled at him, "Sure. How can I say no to that offer?"

Kevin stood up, "Well, okay then. It's a date. How about five thirty. I promise it will be great."

She stood up with him and said, "Okay, I'll be there."

She took her laptop inside and cleaned up what little mess she made. *Wow, he is unbelievable. He is so unlike Edward and much more adorable*, she thought to herself as she walked upstairs to her room to take a shower and get ready for bed. It was already nine and she was exhausted from the trip. She figured she could get up early and take a run and get to work.

She had a couple of dreams that woke her up in the night as she cried. Of course, both dreams were about the girl Brandi Stevens. But other than that, she had gotten a pretty good night's sleep. She went downstairs and made a quick pot of coffee. It was about six thirty and she figured she would have a cup before her run. She wasn't in a hurry. As she grabbed her ipod, she also snatched her phone just in case. She started to run and as she watched the ocean waves, listened to her music and smelled the ocean air, she immediately felt lighter than she had been. It was a pick me up for Laura. Thoughts and ideas were flowing like a tidal wave for her clients. As she came back through, she saw Kevin sitting on his deck drinking his coffee. She pulled out her ear buds and waved. "Good morning Kevin."

He smiled, "Good morning Laura. Did you have a good run?"

"Yes thank you". "I hope you're ready for dinner this evening", he said teasingly.

Laura smiled, "Yes, I am. I will see you later." She walked up the steps and decided to grab some water and then another cup of coffee. She noticed there was a text from Adam.

She called him. That girl was still on her mind. "Hi Adam".

"I hope you had a good night there by yourself."

"Oh, I did. It's just beautiful here."

Laura said, "Oh, yeah. I met your next door neighbor, Kevin. Very nice guy."

Adam agreed, "Oh yes, he is great. He loves the kids when we are there. Always has goodies for them. Spoils them always."

"Can you do me a favor Adam?"

"Sure, what is it?"

"Well, before I left my house, I went into Edward's office to look around. I'm not sure what I was looking for but I ended up finding a deposit slip for a million dollars. On the back of the slip it has a woman's name on it. A Brandi Stevens. Could you look more into this for me? I went running this morning and I have a ton of ideas for our client so I need to get to it before I lose it."

"Yes, sure kiddo. I will check that out for you. Let me know if you run into any problems. I'm glad you are able to relax and get some fresh air."

"Yes. Thanks again, Adam."

As she started working on this Fine Design account, she called Sue who was the CEO and ran a few things by her. Sue was elated by all the new ideas. "You, my lady are a genius. Where did you come up with these ideas?" Sue asked.

Laura loving the approval just said, "Well, when you can back up from the table long enough to regroup, fresh ideas come around and that's when you can pull yourself back in."

Laura had gotten so busy, she had forgotten about having any lunch. And by that time it was already four. "Gosh, I need to go up and shower and get ready for my date", she said to herself. She closed her computer and ran upstairs and hopped in the shower. When she came back in the bedroom with the towel wrapped around, she pulled out some possible outfits. She was looking for sexy but casual.

"Oh, this one is perfect." She chose a baby blue colored simple sun dress. It was backless and very cute. The color looked great with her dark features. She did grab most of her valuable jewelry as she did not want Edward or anyone else to take any of it. She had a very valuable collection which she bought herself. She grabbed her pearl necklace and earrings to match. "Perfect", she said.

CHAPTER THREE

She put on her sandals and started over to Kevin's. He made sure the patio doors were open for her. As she climbed the stairs she could smell something delightful. She walked in, "Hi Kevin. How is it going in here?" Laura asked.

"Oh hi. It's fine. Can I interest you in a glass of wine?"

"Sure", Laura agreed.

"Would you like red or white?"

Laura thought for a moment, "I think white."

He poured her a glass and refreshed his. "It's pretty much done but let's go out and enjoy a cocktail before dinner".

He handed Laura her glass and she followed him outside. They sat down and both sipped.

Laura smiled at him, "Thanks again, Kevin for inviting me over. This was really sweet".

"Well, I couldn't resist. I see this beautiful woman next door to me that looked like an angel. What am I supposed to do? Ignore you? No way." That just made Laura blush and smile.

So, as they drank their wine, Kevin really wanted to know more about Laura but was afraid to ask.

"Laura, I know you didn't want to talk about it but I am a curious person. Why are you here?"

The smile on Laura's face disappeared. "My husband is cheating on me and now we are getting a divorce. It's pretty cut and dry and I don't want to talk about it. I'm sorry."

Kevin moved closer and grabbed her hand, "Why are you sorry? I'm sorry. That is just ridiculous. He is cheating on you? Well, then the man needs a wake-up call because you are amazing. I hope you know that. He stood up and still holding her hand said, Shall we?"

They went inside to eat. He had set up candles on the table and it was all very romantic. The food he prepared was delicious.

"How did you learn to cook like this Kevin? I'm surprised."

"Well, I used to be a chef for a prominent restaurant working for my dad but then moved on to bigger and better things."

Laura looked at him, "Like?"

"Well, now I own that restaurant and also own two more and have some amazing chefs working for me. They are the key to my successful businesses. I take very good care of them."

"Wow. That is impressive" Laura added.

As they ate, drank and talked about a lot of different things, she started to feel strangely close to Kevin. He was such a warm and intelligent person. It was nice having a conversation with a good looking gentleman. Laura had not felt like this since Joe. Her soul mate. She never had feelings like this for Edward. *"I'm an idiot for marrying Edward in the first place."* she thought to herself. All through the evening, Kevin kept getting a little closer to her. As they were both cleaning up in the kitchen, Kevin accidently brushed up against her and smelled Laura's perfume which immediately turned him on. He stood about a foot taller than Laura. He couldn't help it. He grabbed her hips and leaned down and kissed her. She went with it. Laura was all in.   It had been way too long for her. Kevin had seen her body as she ran on the beach and wanted to touch her breasts so badly. Kevin pulled away.

"I am so sorry Laura. You just smell so damn good and you look even better."

Laura grabbed him this time and said, "Please don't be sorry. I like what I see too." And they kissed passionately.

Kevin scooped Laura up in his arms and took her into the living room. He felt that it might be too soon to take her in his bedroom. He laid her down on the couch and he unbuttoned his shirt which exposed his tight chest and six pack stomach. *Oh…my gosh*, is all Laura could think. *Is this too soon? What will he think of me? Will he tell Adam?"* As all these thoughts are running through her mind, she couldn't have been more aroused. *I deserve this damn it*! She tried to rationalize but it was too much. Kevin was kissing her neck and down to her cleavage. He wanted to get in there so badly.

He whispered, "Can I pull this off of you?"

Laura sat up and he pulled her dress over her head and tossed it aside. He wanted to rip her bra and panties off but thought he was moving a little too fast. She grabbed his waistband and unbuttoned his shorts and slowly un-zippered them so that they fell down to his knees as he was kneeling next to her.

He found the back of her bra and it slid off exposing her full breasts and her hard nipples. Kevin went after them, licking and caressing and lightly biting her nipples. He couldn't get enough of them. And she reached down and pulled down his boxer briefs that made him look so tight and hot. She grabbed his long, thick penis and started stroking it. Kevin had his fingers already in her as he playfully licked her nipples.

He looked at her, "I have to have you right now."

And he ripped her panties down and shoved himself inside her and it made Laura gasp.

"Oh my god, Kevin...slow down."

He tried so hard to slow down but it was too late. I'm sorry...........Oh............yeah, yeah, yeah." And within seconds he had finished inside her. He was completely satisfied but left Laura laying there wondering what just happened.

"I apologize Laura. I haven't had sex in so long."

Laura rubbed her hands over her face, "No, it's okay. I guess you needed it worse than me." And she gave him a little smile.

"Please give me another chance Laura. I want you to come on me" and he gave her a wicked smile and started kissing her all over again. Laura thought to herself, *I'm so turned on right now. Maybe this is wrong and I should just leave.* And then Kevin interrupted her thoughts.

"Can I take you into my bedroom? I think we'd be more comfortable in there."

So, he picked her up and took her upstairs and flopped her on his bed and immediately started back into her. There was no warning, he just shoved it inside her. He rolled her on top of him so she could ride him hard. And as she got into mode, he played with her breasts like no one ever had. It was that, that brought her to orgasm almost immediately.

She wanted more. "I want more" and again she started riding him wildly as he licked her nipples at the same time, she came and came and came again. At that point, he couldn't wait another minute. He rolled her back over and this time took his time and enjoyed every thrust and made it count.

It took a lot of self-control as she felt so good. "I love this", he yelled out as he came. She felt the throbbing of his penis as he came so wildly into her. "God, that is so good", Kevin said as he laid next to her. "I have never had a sex that amazing before. Give me five minutes and I want you again." Kevin got up and grabbed glasses of water for them both.

When he entered the bedroom, Laura was under the sheets sitting up.

"You know, I should probably get going as I have to work tomorrow." Laura was a little embarrassed by what happened. Kevin sat down next to her.

"Laura, please don't think that this is what I invited you over for. It just happened that way. I swear my intention was only to spend a dinner and have conversation with a beautiful woman this evening."

She smiled and sighed, "Well, it was my fault as well. Now, I feel like a total slut." Hearing her say that made her laugh.

 Kevin looked at her with a puzzling smile, "What? Did I miss something?"

She nodded, "No. I just have never been the slut before". And she brushed back her hair.

"You are not a slut because that would make me one as well.

"Could you please grab my clothes Kevin?"

"Really? You are set on leaving?"

"I have to. There is too much work to do for my client tomorrow. I have a conference call at eleven and I need to be of sound mind."

Kevin stood up, "I understand." As he stood up, she looked at his amazingly hard body. She thought to herself, *He certainly takes great care of himself and I don't think he's my age at all.*

He had her clothes when he came back in and laid them on the bed next to her and gave her a passionate kiss. She pulled her dress over her and didn't worry about her bra and panties, "Can I ask you a question?" she didn't wait for an answer "How old are you?"

"Does age matter to you?" Kevin asked.

"No not really but you seem so mature and together I would have pegged you for thirty five or so but there is something about you that says you're not even thirty."

"Well, if it is that important to you, I am twenty eight."

Laura felt disgusted and sick to her stomach. *What kind of mistake did I just make?* She thought to herself.

She started walking to the bedroom door to head downstairs, "Kevin, I feel horrible about all of this. I'm sorry."

He came over to her and with a smirk said, "Well, I don't feel horrible and I'm not sorry." Laura just wanted to get out of there.

"Thank you for the evening. I guess I'll see you around." And before she could take a step out onto the deck, he grabbed her and kissed her.

"Please don't run away from me. I really like you. Age is nothing to be afraid of."

And with that she headed down the stairs and over to her temporary home. She thought, *Age is something to be afraid of. He hasn't even gotten a clue about love. It's all about sex with him.*

So, she showered to try and feel clean and went to check her emails but figured she would just get a fresh jump on it in the morning. All that sex, was like another work out. She smiled with that thought. *I haven't had sex like that........ever.* And she drifted off to sleep feeling very satisfied.

CHAPTER FOUR

When Laura woke up the next morning, she went down to make her coffee and was trying to decide if she felt up to running. She talked herself into a walk after she had a few cups of coffee. As she grabbed her laptop and her cup, she opened the French doors to the deck. The ocean breeze hit her right away and gave her a feeling of freedom and a fresh start. She sat down and started looking at what other adventures she could participate in while she was there. *I could go hiking in the mountains this weekend. It's a ride but it looks amazing.* She looked over and didn't see any movement next door. His doors were still closed to the deck. She was a little nervous now as there would be nothing that could come out of this. It was just sex...........nothing more. Laura wanted a relationship. Not with Kevin. With someone that had more than sex on his mind. After coffee and emails, she looked at the time. It was eight am. *I'll take a walk and be*

refreshed for my conference call at eleven.
She grabbed her phone and ipod and started walking along the beach.

As she walked she thought to herself, *I'm really going to have to figure out where I'll be staying once I'm back in New York. I'm not sure if I'll have any luck finding an apartment or condo in my price range and in a desirable area. I'll have to speak with Adam about that.* Then she prepped herself for the conference call with her clients. She wasn't worried, she had already run the ideas through the CEO who loved them. Now it was just answering any questions the rest of the company's heads might want to know.

When she got back in and prepared herself, she called Adam to see if he wanted to join in on the call. "Hi Adam."

"Hey kiddo, how are you holding up?"

"Fine. I have a conference call at eleven with Fine Design's company heads. Do you want in?"

"Actually, Laura. I have an appointment at eleven. I need to speak with you AFTER your call. I don't want to upset you beforehand."

Laura feeling nauseated asked, "It's about Edward? And his little floozy?"

"Yes, but this conversation can wait another hour. Call me as soon as you are done and I'll conference you in so the attorney, Jack Larson, can talk to you. He has a few questions for you."

"Okay Adam" and they hung up.

As soon as the conference call was through, she immediately phoned Adam. "Okay Laura, you're now live with Jack and I."

"Now, what did you find out about this Brandi girl?" was the first words out of Laura's mouth.

Adam said, "Well, she is twenty two years old and not only did your husband deposit money into an account for her, he also bought her a penthouse so he had somewhere to stay with her. It was close to his office as well." There was silence. Laura thought she was going to be sick.

And then Adam asked "Laura? Are you okay?"

Jack interrupted, "Laura, we have a lot of financial statements and it looks to me that he has a lot of accounts overseas and investments all over the place. Not only are we going to get this divorce for you, I also have a colleague working on the financial end of it as that is what he specializes in. So, right now, Edward is being scrutinized and a lot of his accounts, including Brandi's is frozen to make certain that he makes no sudden moves. Now that we have contacted him to notify that we are representing you, the natural instinct is to start moving funds around. I'm sure he already has done that but we are limiting him for anything further."

Laura asked, "My account is okay though?"

"Yes, we left the accounts with only your name on them open."

She sighed…….."Oh good."

It's too bad this is happening to the Jennings name. His father would be turning over in his grave right now if he knew what was happening. I knew Charles Jennings very well. Now Laura, I want to keep the lines of communication open so we can move through this quickly so you can move forward", Jack said.

"Yes, no problem. You can reach me whenever you or your colleagues may have questions."

Adam then added in, "One thing is for sure Laura, Edward may be in deep. You will be set for life as long as you don't leave this firm. I and the company need you."

That made Laura laugh, "Don't worry Adam, I'm not going anywhere." Jack asked, "Do you have any more questions for me?"

"No. I'm sure Edward has accounts hidden everywhere. Maybe even using aliases. He is very smart."

Jack Larson responded, "Again, my colleague will be searching for anything off."

"Mr. Larson I appreciate it and thank you for moving so quickly."

"Well, when Adam called me and told me, I knew we needed to jump on this. If you have any questions at all, please don't hesitate to call and if I'm not available, leave a message and I'll get back to you as soon as I can."

Once she was off the phone, she cried. "Twenty two years old?" she sobbed to herself. "What is he thinking? I know what she is thinking, money. I was dumped for a twenty two year old. Unbelievable." Laura started to get angry. She didn't know what she wanted to do with herself now. She looked at the clock, well its twelve fifteen, time for a drink. So, she grabbed herself a beer and sat outside with no computer or no phone. After she had a couple, she saw Kevin step out onto his deck. He looked over and saw her.

"Starting a little early aren't you?"

"I have every right to. I have had the worst news and I'm a little angry right now."

He asked, "Do you feel like company?"

She thought for a few seconds,
"Yeah…………I guess." So, he ran over.

She looked at him, "grab a beer if you want
and grab me another as well."

When Kevin came back out with their beers, he
asked, "What happened?"

"Well, my husband, soon to be ex, was fucking
a twenty two year old. And not only that, he
had deposited a couple of million into her
account AND bought her a penthouse close to
his office so he could go over there whenever
he wanted to screw the little floozy."

Kevin shook his head in disgust, "I'm so sorry
Laura. He sounds like a real slime. A typical
power-head."

She ran her fingers through her hair, "Yeah,
but the attorneys are on it." She smiled, "They
froze the little bitches account and most of his.
Sweet justice will be served." And she looked
over at Kevin after she said it, "I'm not a
spiteful person. But for how he treated me and
for the years of my life that he has taken from
me, I have a right to feel this vicious."

"I agree with you Laura. What a jerk. I have
never treated a woman like that."

She looked at him and now that the alcohol
was kicking in she said, "Really? I figured you
were just a sex fiend."

Kevin looked offended, "No, I told you last night that I wasn't expecting to have sex with you. I'm sorry about that. Now your just making me feel like a monster."

She felt bad, "Oh gosh Kevin, I didn't mean for it to come out like that."

He looked at her and said, "Listen, I'm pretty sure that you have not had anything to eat yet today. Let's grab some take out and we'll come back here and eat. You'll feel better after you eat. There is a place down the road where we can get tasty wraps. We'll walk. It's not that far."

So, Laura grabbed her shoes and keys and they headed out. She was still feeling a good buzz going. "Kevin, I'm thirty six years old. I'm getting divorced and I like you. But I just feel that it would never work between us. You are still so young."

He stopped and looked at her, "There is a lot of things you don't know about me. I grew up quickly. And maybe to you the age difference is scary but if I had to put an age on myself maturity wise it would be about forty." They started to walk again.

"What has happened in your life that you feel this way Kevin?" He shook his head, "You know.............it's just not something I want to talk about right now."

"Okay" Laura said and they dropped it.

They came back to her place and she grabbed a couple of glasses of water and they sat outside and ate.

"Wow, these are really good wraps". Between the walk and now food in Laura's stomach, she started to feel better.

"Please don't think I'm a bad person. I'm just a normal person that is going through some bad things. That's why I'm here. You just complicated things a bit." But she smiled when she said it.

Kevin grabbed her hand, "Oh I complicated things? I think you are the one who did that. Coming in here and running past my home in your little outfit. Are you kidding me?" He said teasingly and he gave her a kiss.

"Well, I won't be here this weekend so, you'll be free of me."

"Where are you going? You're not going back to New York yet are you?" Kevin started to panic.

"No, I'm going hiking in the mountains. I found a group thing and signed up. It will be good for me."

Kevin agreed, "Oh yeah…………it's beautiful there. You will have fun."

"You will, however, miss out on my little party. I thought I would get everyone together so that you could meet some of my friends and realize that I'm not such a bad guy."

"Oh, I didn't know. I could cancel but I was looking forward to it."

Kevin looked at her and said, "No, you go. I'll postpone the party for next weekend or have another one."

"Well, what if I end up leaving before next weekend?"

He grabbed her face and said, "I need you here a little longer" and he kissed her passionately, sending electricity up her inner thighs. He whispered into her ear, "Can I have you right now? I've been thinking about you all morning and it's killing me."

By that time, she was feeling so aroused. They walked into the house and right into the living room. Again, he immediately disrobed her and himself and turned her over on all fours. He didn't need any foreplay, he was ready to go. He shoved himself inside her and she moaned. It was pain with pleasure. He started into her grabbing on to her hips. It was like he couldn't get enough. Laura screamed out for him to slow down but he couldn't, he grabbed her hair. "I want it so bad. You have no idea what you do to me Laura. Let me come..................oh yeah......." He pushed it deep inside her but he wasn't done. He turned her over and made her straddle him.

She started riding and he was ready to go again. He played with her nipples as she started going crazy, he knew she was going to orgasm as she plunged his erection deeper into her and then she cried out, "I'm coming…………..I'm coming." And then there were fire in her eyes. She looked at him, "I want more" and she took it.

She came on him over and over again until he couldn't hold off any longer, and came with her pulling her hips down on him until they collapsed in a sweaty mass. Sex with her was like never wanting to quit. Like a very dangerous drug that made you powerless under its intoxication. Laura was that drug. Kevin started to feel powerless under her. He just couldn't get enough of her body.

When they were done, they laid next to each other. He took in her beautiful body. She was perfect. Laura actually fell asleep and Kevin covered her with a blanket and went back to his place while she rested. He felt bad for what she was going through and wanted her to sleep for a little while. *She'll feel better when she wakes up* he thought to himself. He figured he would check in on her in about an hour or so.

When she awoke, she felt like she just ran a marathon. She heard her phone ringing. *I feel like crap*, she thought as she scrambled for her phone. She looked at the caller id, "Yes, Edward. What's the problem?" She was very curt with him.

Edward was furious. "What are you trying to do to me? All my accounts are frozen."

"I didn't do anything. Adam found me an attorney and the attorney is the one who did that. He told me it was part of the process."

He was trying to be calm but Laura could hear the panic in his voice. "Listen, Laura. I'm sorry all this happened but I need access to my accounts so I will propose something so that you can call off the dogs. I will give you twenty five million dollars and we both walk away with no attorneys involved. We get the divorce papers signed, sit in front of the judge and we go our own ways."

Laura was upset with the way he was just acting like their marriage was just a business transaction. She thought to herself, *He doesn't even care what happens to me.* "I will speak to the attorneys and see what I can do. I do however have one question I need to ask you."

Edward replied hesitantly, "Go ahead".

"Did you ever love me? Are you even capable of loving anyone or anything? Do you even care about what I'm going through?"

There was silence and then Edward answered, "I'm not sure if I loved you. I think I did when we got married and I do care about you but I guess I'm unable to be a husband to anyone. Where are you anyhow?"

Laura fought back tears and simply said, "I am working out of the city right now. I will get back to you as soon as I speak to the attorney but I'm not sure that will help. It's an investigation and they have to follow protocol. By the way……I know about Brandi. Good bye Edward."

"What a jerk!!" she said aloud.

And just as she said that, she heard a voice behind her "Who's a jerk?" It was Kevin.

She wrapped the blanket around her and still pissed said, "Edward. The heartless asshole wants to buy me out of the divorce. It's because all of his accounts were frozen. But what he doesn't know is they will remain frozen regardless because they found some issues with financial statements they found." Kevin walked closer to her and sat down.

"Well, what are you going to do?"

She shook her head, "Nothing. I will tell my attorneys what Edward said but they have to follow protocol if they are investigating his accounts. I can't do anything about it." She looked at him, "Let me go upstairs and get some clothes on. Do you feel like taking a walk with me?"

"Yeah sure" Kevin agreed.

They took a nice long walk and by that time it started to get later. It was around seven pm and they were both hungry.

"Can I take you out to eat? There is a place down the way that is very good." Kevin asked.

"Sounds good. It can't be a late night for me. I still have to get ready for tomorrow morning. I figured, I would just hit a store up that way for water and snacks and a backpack."

CHAPTER FIVE

The next day, Laura was to get moving early to go to the mountains for her hike with the group. They were meeting at nine o'clock. She figured if she left around six, she would have enough time to stop at the store first. It was a couple hours' drive to the mountains or where she was going anyway. As she drove, she listened to the voice on the gps. It was now eight fifteen and she pulled into a Target store. The first thing she did was grab a back pack and headed over to the grocery section. As she was in the snack isle looking for a good trail mix, she looked over and thought she saw someone familiar. She didn't mean to stare but he then looked over.

"Joe? Joe Vinetti?" He walked over to Laura.

"Oh my gosh….Laura Brooks".

He gave her a big hug. "What are you doing here? This is so weird bumping into you like this." She smiled. He still looked the same and she looked down at his finger to look for a ring. There was none. "I'm actually staying two hours from here on the coast. My boss and friend lent me out his vacation home. I'm meeting up with a hiking group today."

Joe asked her, "So, how have you been? Are you married? Do you have kids?"

Laura shook her head, "No kids and no husband. The husband part is a long story and I don't have enough time. What about you?"

Joe said, "Well, I'm divorced and I have one three year old daughter, Genevieve." He pulled a picture out of his wallet.

"Oh, she is so sweet Joe. You are very lucky."

"Laura, it has been so long. And since you are up here, why don't you skip the hike and spend the day with me so we can catch up. I'll take you for a hike. Just you and me. I mean how weird is it that we bumped into each other?"

Laura was loving that idea. "Really? You don't have anything else to do today?" Her heart was pumping a little faster than usual. She actually felt like a nervous school girl.

"Nope. Genevieve is with her mom this weekend. I was just going to get some things to throw on the grill today. Wow, it's been how long since we've seen each other Laura?"

"It's been about eight years or so." She replied. "Can I take a rain check on that offer Joe?"

And he immediately replied uncomfortably, "Oh, sure….no problem"

Laura felt bad, "I'm sorry. I just don't want to blow off the group when they are expecting me."

Joe smiled, "I understand. They'll be waiting for you. Why don't we exchange numbers and go from there. You will be here for a while I hope?"

"Oh yes. My boss was nice enough to let me work from his vacation home on the beach. I would love to catch up with you though."

And with that, Laura gave him a hug and grabbed what she needed and off she went.

That whole day was a blur to her. All she thought of was Joe. The one true love that got away. Her soul mate that she should have ended up with instead of the asshole that she married and is in the mess she in now. Why did she blow Joe off today? She should have spent the day with him. She couldn't stop thinking about him. How weird it was that she ran into him.

The hike was over and she got into her car. As she drove back to the coast, all she thought about was Joe. *He looked so good,* she thought to herself. *Maybe I'll give him a call tomorrow and see what he's doing.*

When she pulled into the driveway, she saw Kevin out on his deck with some friends. *Oh....great*, She thought to herself. *I don't feel like going over there and dealing with Kevin right now.*

As she got out of the car, he waved over at her and started down the stairs. "Hey, you want to join the party?"

"Not really Kevin. I'm really tired and I'm going to bed. I'll talk to you tomorrow".

"Oh, C'mon. Just for a little while?" and Kevin grabbed her and tried to kiss her.

She backed off and pleaded with him, "Please Kevin. I'm exhausted. Go have fun with your friends." And she headed towards the house as he stood there watching her disappointed.

As she threw everything down on the chair, she checked her phone and it was about ten sixteen pm and she thought about calling Joe to see what his plans were for tomorrow. She figured he'd still be up since he didn't have his daughter. *What the hell*, she thought. So she looked him up and pressed dial.

Her stomach was so nervous it felt like there were finger tips tickling her from inside. He answered. "Hi, Joe. I hope it's not too late but I wanted to know what your plans were for tomorrow."

He replied, "I just have to pick Genevieve up after dinner tomorrow."

"Could I come up and maybe grab some lunch for us so we can catch up for a little while? It's fine if you're busy. We can do it some other time."

"No. That sounds great. I'll be here so whenever you get here it's fine. I'll text you my address."

Laura trying to hold back her excitement replied, "okay, I'll see you tomorrow then." And hung up waiting for his text.

She ran up and grabbed a shower and thought about tomorrow. *This is a second chance. Maybe.* She thought. *I'm getting ahead of myself.*

She poured herself a glass of wine and relaxed for a little while hoping she didn't get a visit from Kevin again. *He is way too young for me. I need to see where this goes between Joe and I first before I let Kevin think there is anything going on between us.*

She fell asleep and had dream after dream and awoke refreshed and full of excitement and thinking it was going to be a good day.

She got up and put on some coffee and got dressed. She threw some make-up on and did what she could with her hair and came back down to grab a quick cup of coffee and check her emails. She didn't want to leave too late. It was already seven thirty and it takes a couple of hours to get there. She sent Joe a text when she left just to let him know her approximate time of arrival.

It was a small ranch home. Probably two thousand square feet if that she figured. It was very well kept. The front had nice big pillars going into the house and had double doors for the entrance. *"It is so freaking weird that I ran into Joe. What are the chances of that happening?"* Laura wondered to herself as she walked to the door. It was kind of weird that she was spending the day with him after not seeing him after all these years. She knocked and he answered. "Hi Laura"

"Are you sure you want to spend the day with me?" Laura asked uncomfortably.

"Laura, how coincidental is it that we bumped into each other? I'm not usually in the store that early in the day. It was almost meant to be. Of course I want to catch up."

She was relieved that he felt that way. *Gosh, he looks good. It should have been him that I married,* "she thought. He took her into the house and gave her a tour. Little Genevieve's room was adorable. All pinks and purples with some green worked in. "Totally princess" Laura said smiling.

He agreed, "Yeah, she is my little princess."

"If you don't mind me asking, what happened to you and your wife?" Joe rubbed is chin, "Hmmm, well, we got married because we found out she was pregnant but we weren't really compatible. It was just one of those things. We get along great but we are more friends than anything else. At least I got Genevieve out of it."

"What about you? What's your story? If you don't mind me asking." And he smiled at her.

"Well, it's a long story and it all just happened so you are going to have to excuse my anger and any emotions that may emerge."

He grabbed her hand. "Let's go sit outside on the deck and get comfortable and then you can tell me." So, she followed him outside, she found a chair and sat.

She took a deep breath and continued, "Well, I was married or am married for not much longer. I met Edward five years ago and have been married for almost four. I should have seen all the signs. He is not capable of loving anyone. I wanted a baby and he kept saying no and then I find out that he is cheating on me with some twenty two year old. He bought a twenty five million dollar penthouse for her AND deposited a couple million dollars into her account. That is why I am out here. It just happened and I'm still a little bitter from the whole ordeal."

"Laura, I am so sorry. Only a real jerk could do something like that." She shook her head, "You know? The only thing I'm really upset about is that he took five years of my life away that I can't possibly get back. I could have married someone worthy and who truly loved me and wanted to have a family with me. I'll be fine though. I'm tough."

Joe moved his chair a little closer to her. "So, what is it that you do for a living? What does Edward do that he has millions of dollars to throw around like that?"

She was amused by the way he asked her, "I am an executive with Fusion, Inc. in New York and Edward is an investor and an investment broker for Preston, Inc. But his dad set the path for him so he didn't really have to work all that hard to get where he is. He had a huge leg up. What do you do Joe?"

He laughed, "Well, nothing compared to what you do. I work on aircraft and am the head supervisor." He waited for a response and looked at Laura. She was in deep thought. "Laura? Are you okay? Did I shock you?"

She smiled at him. "No. I'm sorry. Sounds like you really enjoy your job."

"Yeah, I guess. So basically, we both made some pretty bad decisions after we left one another" Joe said. "What happened there anyhow? Can you refresh my memory?"

"Hmmm, well, you basically freaked out and thought that the next step in our relationship was marriage even though we had never brought it up. You stopped coming home and not discussing it with me so I had thought that you were cheating. I started going out with my friends and met someone that ended up being a total loser but when you found out you begged for me back. You kept saying you were sorry and to give you another chance. But because I was afraid you would leave me again, I said no which was probably the worst mistake of my life and I've regretted it ever since."

"Oh yeah.............now I remember. I was staying at my cousin's house, I never cheated on you. I'm really sorry that I didn't come to you first and talk about it. I am a real idiot."

"Well, it's water under the bridge. We both were at fault for what happened. I'm just glad we ran into each other and are able to catch up. I'm still shocked that we would run into each other though. Do you realize that I have thought about you pretty much every day since we went our separate ways?" Laura said.

"Really? I have wondered where and what you have been up to as well."

Joe stood up and grabbed her hand to pull her up with him. "Can I at least take you for that hike that I promised you?"

"Yes, that would be great. Let me grab my back pack and we'll throw a bunch of snacks and drinks in there." So Laura ran out to her car to grab everything. Joe turned to look at her coming through the door.

"Can I just tell you that you look just as good if not better than you did eight years ago? But you were always a knock out."

Flattered Laura teased, "Well thank you for that. And I have to say you look pretty good yourself. You still have your hair and I can see you stay fit."

Joe nodded, "I get to work-out at the gym at work. It's free."

Laura said, "I run. That's free as well." And they both laughed.

After they packed everything up, they got into his truck and took off. "There is a trail right down the road about ten minutes away. That way we can hike and be home so that I can make us lunch."

Laura started searching for a rubber band for her hair and said, "Sounds good to me." Joe showed Laura some beautiful spots. The one she loved best was the falls that were secluded and it looked like such a mystical place. "I wish I would have brought my camera. This is awesome."

Joe nudged her and said, "Well, maybe if you stick around a couple more weeks, I can take you back in there and to a couple of other trails that have some amazing scenes."

"That could be a possibility. I have the ability to work from anywhere so my boss's vacation home is available to me for as long as I want. He basically kicked me out. He told me I worked too much and I had no life and he didn't want me in there."

Joe thought that was funny, "Wow, what a boss. I wish I had a boss like that."

The only thing is, I will have to go back to New York to sit in front of the judge for our divorce. I'm not sure when that will be. Have you ever been to New York City?"

"Only once. But it was when I was very young."

"Well, maybe you can come back with me for a few days."

"I would love to be able to do that Laura but I don't get a lot of vacation time off through my job, unfortunately." They found somewhere to sit and they were both in thought.

As they pulled out the trail mix and the bottled water, Joe leaned in and gave Laura a kiss. "I am just amazed to be sitting here with you. I have thought a lot about you through the years but didn't know if I should even try to contact you."

Laura said, "Well, I will admit that I knew that you were in California. I just didn't know where and if you were or weren't married." After they sat for a while talking, they decided to head back to the truck.

They got back to Joe's house and they both started working on a late lunch. "I am going to have to get going after we eat so that you can get your daughter. But I would like to get together again" Laura said.

Joe actually looked disappointed, "Of course. I just wish you could stay for a while longer. I had a nice time today. I could actually check with my ex to see if she could take Genevieve next weekend too and I'll take her the next two weekends."

Laura smiled at him and asked, "She would actually do that for you?"

"Oh yeah. We have a good relationship. It's not like you think most of divorces are like. It's not like yours will be. Not even close."

Laura replied, "Well, maybe you can come to the beach house with me next weekend if that happens. It would be fun."

Joe looked at her, "That would be great."

Laura now realizing that Joe was still living the way she lived with her parents and understood that he probably didn't have a whole lot of money to do things like stay at the beach or travel. "Yeah, we'll grab breakfast in the morning. Have cocktails on the deck overlooking the ocean. It will be relaxing. I'm sure you could use some of that."

After they ate, Laura started cleaning and Joe was loading the dishwasher and said, "I feel like we haven't skipped a beat. It doesn't feel like we missed out on the last eight years of one another. We just picked up where we left off."

Laura came over and hugged him, "No. It doesn't. Just let me know about next weekend and if not, we'll plan for the weekend after."

Joe leaned over and kissed her. It sent electricity through her. She looked up at him and smiled, "Wow, I definitely miss that."

"It's amazing", Joe said. And Laura looked at him puzzled. And he finished his thought, "It's amazing how we take so much for granted. When that one person who fit so perfectly in my heart and soul I just let walk away." And Laura and gave him the biggest hug.

"That is so sweet Joe. It's okay. If it's meant to be. It will happen. I have so much on my plate right now. I can't really think about a serious relationship. Let's catch up first. Let me know about the weekend."

Joe walked her out to her car and gave her another hug and that one last kiss. It was a passionate one that sent a sensation that started from her chest and slowly moved down to her stomach through her thighs stopping at her knees where they wanted to buckle underneath her.

He looked at her, "I sure hope that Jen takes Genevieve next weekend. I would love to spend the whole weekend kissing you." That just made her melt.

"Just let me know and it can be arranged" and Laura smiled.

She got into her car and put the gps on, waved and off she went her heart beating so fast she had to use her breathing techniques to bring her heart rate down. *Phew.........I am NOT ready for that. Or am I? I still have to deal with an ugly divorce and alimony hearing which is going to be pretty messy. I can't put him through that.*

CHAPTER SIX

When she got back to the beach house, it was around six thirty. She knew Kevin would be on the lookout for her and more than likely popping in. *He is NOT seducing me this time*, she thought to herself. This thing between us is over.

She went inside and changed to go take a walk along the beach. As soon as she walked out, there was Kevin. He ran out after her.

"Hey, Laura. I was looking for you today."

"Yeah, I ran into a longtime friend I haven't seen in about eight years so I spent the day with him."

Kevin looked at her in disbelief as he walked along with her, "Him?" he asked.

"Yes, Kevin. Him. His name is Joe. Do I need to tell you everything that goes on in my life?"

"Well, is he a boyfriend or something?"

"Yes Kevin, he is an old boyfriend. Can we drop the subject so I can take a nice relaxing walk please?"

Kevin was in deep thought. "Well since you'll be working all week, I thought I might cook dinner and bring it over since you never take a break to eat all day."

"Sure, that would be nice. Just let me know what days so I'm prepared as some of my calls run late."

"Okay good." And with that Kevin turned around and jogged back to his house and Laura was relieved she could finish her walk in peace and quiet.

The next morning she was up and working away and Joe was on her mind. Every time her phone rang, she was hoping it was him telling her it was a go for the weekend. She worked late into Monday evening and told Kevin that it wasn't a good day for dinner. She just grabbed herself a sandwich and iced tea and worked until about eight. And then ended up falling asleep on the couch.

Tuesday morning came along and she awoke startled. Kevin came in and gave her a kiss and was sitting next to her. "Kevin! What in the hell are you doing in here?"

"You, Miss, left the door unlocked."

"That doesn't mean you just come on in here and scare the shit out of me like that!" Laura shouted. "Geez Kevin"

"Sorry", Kevin apologized. "I brought you a caramel latte. Do I get credit for that? I made sure I got you the largest one they had with skim milk."

"Yes, I'm sorry I yelled at you. You just freakin scared me. Thank you."

Kevin insisted, "I am bringing you dinner tonight. Sandwiches and iced tea do not cut it in my world."

Laura responded, "I guess I have no choice. But I do have to get to work. What time is it anyway?"

"It's eight thirty. You slept in this morning."

"Oh my gosh……….I did sleep in. I really do need to get to work."

"Okay. I'll get out of your way and I'll see you later."

With that Laura, enjoying her latte opened her laptop and started in on work wondering if she was going to hear from Joe today. So, as the day went by and still no Joe, she started to get thwarted by the silence.

Kevin, of course brought over dinner and definitely showed his talent by making a seafood and pasta dish with fresh salad and red wine. It was simple but delicious. They enjoyed it el fresco and had a wonderful meal. "I'm having some friends over this weekend and would like you to come" Kevin said.

"I'll see Kevin. I'm not much for crowds or meeting a lot of new people right now."

"It's not going to be that big. Just a few people. But okay. I'm not going to push you into going if you don't want to partake in a little bit of atmosphere other than yourself."

"Thank you so much for dinner Kevin. It really is quite delicious. You have a real talent."

"Laura, I so feel something for you. I can't help it. I feel a connection to you."

"Please Kevin, I have so much going on right now, I really don't want to get into an even bigger mess than I am in right now. I have to deal with one matter at a time. Plus, the age factor. I don't feel comfortable at all with that."

"I already told you that age doesn't matter to me. Why do you keep bringing that up when it's such an insignificant issue? And what mess? So your husband is an asshole. I can deal with that."

Laura looking totally annoyed and not at all wanting to engage in this conversation simply said, "Look Kevin, this is not something I wish to discuss at this time. It's been a long day and if you can't respect the way I feel and drop it, then you may leave and not speak to me again."

"Wait, Laura. I'm sorry. I do respect the way you feel. But I have feelings too. I will drop it and when you're ready, I'll be waiting."

With that they finished up dinner and went their separate ways even though Kevin was reluctant to leave Laura. He really wanted to spend some more time with her. But he needed to give her some time.

Wednesday came and Laura finally received the phone call she had been waiting for. And she was jumping for joy. Joe was able to get the weekend free. *Woohoo!!!!!* Laura was so excited. That just made the week go by that much faster and her work production was that much more creative. She had something to look forward to.

She went out and grabbed some food to throw in the fridge along with beer and wine. She thought maybe margaritas would be fun to make one night. She grabbed some fresh flowers to spruce the place up. Today was the day. It was Friday and he was coming out right after work. After that kiss last weekend, she didn't know what to expect.

Laura saw lights pull into the driveway. She ran out to greet him.

Joe got out of his truck, "My god, this is great!!! You are so lucky." "Well, let's go up and have a beer or glass of wine and enjoy what we can see of the ocean. Grab your bags and I'll show you around."

As they sat on the deck having some cocktails. Joe felt the ocean breeze and said, "This is just beautiful. What a perfect place to live." She saw Kevin walk out onto his deck and it looked to be maybe four guys and five girls over there. But Kevin looked over and saw Laura sitting with Joe and he didn't even wave or say hi or anything. It looked as if he stormed back into his house.

"Kevin lives next door. He is very nice and he is a great cook."

Joe looked over there. "Did you want to go over?"

"Oh no. It looks as if he has enough people over there." They had a couple more cocktails and talked about the past and the fun times they had with Laura's friends and family functions and all the good memories. They had some good laughs. Laura said to Joe, "Looking back, I feel really bad for you now.

Going to all my family functions. I guess I should be apologizing to you."

Joe just laughed, "No, actually, your brothers were awesome. I loved hanging out with your family. It was always a good time. Crazy but fun. Just like your friends. That was always an experience. We would walk away with a story to tell every time we would go out with them."

"I really want to meet your daughter, Joe. If that's okay. I wanted a baby in the worst way. I was ready to be a mom. Now I feel as if that is all ruined for me." Joe stroked her hair, "I would love for you to meet Genevieve. And it's not too late for you to have children."

"Yeah…..right. By the time I find someone and get married, I'll be too old." He looked straight into her eyes, "I thought you did find someone." And he kissed her passionately.

"Do you want to take this inside?"

He smiled at her, "That sounds good." So, as they both walked in, Laura made sure she shut all the doors and they were locked. She didn't want Kevin walking in like he started doing. She really liked him but knew there was no future between them. He just wanted the sex. She needed something more. Joe and her were and are still perfect for each other. This was fate. She just felt it. They sat on the couch and she turned on the television. But she wasn't thinking movie and she was pretty sure Joe wasn't thinking movie either by his body language.

Joe leaned down and kissed her. He was so gentle. So unlike Kevin. She wasn't complaining at all about what Kevin and she had. It was crazy off-the-wall animal like sex which was good a couple of times but she needed love.

He whispered, "I missed you Laura" That just made her want him more.

"I missed you too" And he started kissing her neck and back up to her lips. There was a warmth that moved through every part of her body.

He started to nibble on her ear, "I just want to feel you again."

Laura looked at him, "But what happens when I leave? How will it work between us?"

"Laura, we bumped into each other for some reason. Let's not ruin this. We will never have another chance."

They moved upstairs. She turned on the stereo and they laid on the bed just kissing and enjoying each other.

Joe looked at Laura, "I could just kiss you all night. We don't have to do anything else if you don't want to." They fondled each other and kissed but nothing else happened. Laura didn't want to complicate things. She wanted him in the worst way but felt it could wait a little longer. She wished now that things didn't happen between her and Kevin. Joe held her all night.

When they awoke the next morning, they started kissing and things started to get out of control. Joe started kissing her working his way down between her legs. He worked her until she came. And then worked his way into her. He slowly slid it inside her and it brought back great memories. Their love making was never dull. Laura could tell that he was doing everything he could not to finish too quickly.

She looked up at him, "Come for me baby" and with those words said, he lost control and picked up the pace, faster and deeper until he yelled out,

"Oh, Laura, Oh yeah. That was so good." And he kissed her deep and whispered in her ear, "god I missed you." And he laid down next to her rubbing her breasts. "And I missed these."

Which made Laura laugh. "Do you want eggs this morning?" She asked.

"Yes, that and coffee." So, they both got up and dressed and headed downstairs. He pulled her close and said, "That was just the preview. I want another go at that after breakfast. You are too sexy."

They sat on the deck with their coffee, eggs and toast when she heard Kevin say, "Good morning" She looked over and he was standing on the deck.

"Oh good morning Kevin." He started walking over to Laura and Joe and walked out to the deck. Laura stood up and said "Kevin, this is my past, Joe and Joe this is Kevin."

Joe stood up and extended his hand, "Nice to meet you." Kevin looked at him and hesitated but ended up shaking his hand, "Nice meeting you too".

Kevin looked at Laura, "so, you go hiking for the day and you end up bringing a guy you meet back the next weekend?"

Laura hearing the malice in his voice said, "No. It's not like that. Joe and I used to be very serious but eight years ago we had a misunderstanding and ended up going our separate ways. When I went into Target to get snacks and drinks for the hike, strangely enough, I ran into Joe. How weird is that? So, we started catching up on old times and the years missed."

"Well, that works out for you two. I guess I'll talk to you later." And Kevin walked back to his house.

Joe looked at Laura a bit confused, "Did I just miss something? He sounded like he wanted to pound me. Did I take something away from him?"

Laura shook her head, "No. no it's nothing like that. I'm not sure what his problem is. That was a little weird though." Joe agreed, "Yeah the intensity in his body language and his eyes were pretty alarming."

"Oh……..he is harmless. He is good friends with my boss. He wouldn't hurt me." So, they finished up their breakfast and Joe looked at Laura.

"Would you join me in the shower?"

She giggled, "Oh yeah? Okay. I'll take that offer."

So they headed upstairs and started the shower. As they undressed, they kissed and explored each other. When they finally got into the shower, they were both so aroused. Joe got in behind her and started playing with her breasts.   He placed her hands on the shower wall and pulled her hips into him as he shoved himself inside her. This one was intense. He couldn't get enough as he started pumping her harder and grabbed her shoulders and then slid his hands to feel her hard nipples which completely had Laura wanting more. She knew he came when he yelled out.

He turned her around to ravish her mouth with a deep kiss. "I just can't get enough of you. I want you to ride me." So, they showered and pleasured each other until they turned the shower off. They dried off and he picked her up off her feet and took her to the bed. He pulled her on top of him and she started to ride him.

She was so ready she came immediately. "I need to come again" and she started back in and she came five more times. By that time Joe couldn't wait. He took his missionary position and went at it trying to get Laura to come again.

 "Oh baby, come for me. I want to come with you" and at that moment of time, Laura screamed out in pleasure and Joe moaned as he finished inside her.

She lay next to him as they both gasped for air. There was silence until Laura asked, "What do you feel like doing today? Do you want to take a walk on the beach?" Joe kissed her and said, "Maybe I just want to stay in bed all day."

She smiled at him, "It's only Saturday morning." And then Joe kissed her and said, "Sure, let's go take a walk and got up to get dressed. Laura was in heaven. His body was amazing. His shoulders, back, arms and abs were so toned, his musculature was perfect. She watched him get dressed before she got up. He was beautiful.

As they started for the beach, Kevin watched their every move. Laura was very aware of his stare downs as was Joe. "Are you sure you feel safe here?"

Joe asked again. "I'm almost getting a stalker feel to this Kevin guy."

Laura shook her head, "No, I think he may be a little jealous of you but he's twenty eight years old. Give me a break."

Laura wanted to change the subject, "So, what do you want to do today?"

Joe looked at her and smiled, "What do you think? No. I just want to spend time with you and hang out on the beach, maybe go swimming with you."

Laura replied, "Fair enough but I'm taking you out to a restaurant down the road later."

When they got back from their walk, they decided to go swimming. Joe could not keep his hands off Laura. She was loving every minute of their time together and thought about how much she missed out on. This is what a relationship should be. They had so much fun swimming and yet she could feel Kevin's eyes burning into her every movement. Laura was starting to feel very uncomfortable. But Joe was also noticing it as well and was feeling uneasy about the whole situation.

"Laura, I'm just sensing that this guy is not on the up and up and I fear he may do something to you. He's a stalker Laura."

"Yeah, he's starting to freak me out a little too. I guess I'll have to have a talk with him after you leave."

Joe got upset, "After I leave? No. Before I leave because if he hurts you, I'm going to whip his ass. The little punk doesn't know who he's dealing with."

"Okay. I'll talk to him before we have lunch."

So after they were done swimming, they came up to the house and Joe stood on the deck while Laura went over to speak to Kevin.

Kevin was very Curt to her, "What do you need?"

"Kevin, why are watching my every move? It's making me very uncomfortable."

"Oh is it? Well good because you had some good excuses for not wanting to pursue a relationship with me but you look awfully affectionate with Joey. BULL SHIT....It was all bull shit Laura"

"Look Kevin, It's much more involved than that. We go way back and I've known him for years. I've known you for days. You THINK you love me and you are only twenty eight years old.

Joe and I had a relationship before so I know how things were and where they should have gone. And I shouldn't have to explain my life to you. Please stop obsessing over me."

"This is not over Laura. I will fight for you. I will show you I love you somehow, some way. I can promise you that." And Laura saw the desperation and the look of pleading in his eyes and had to look away.

Laura finally turned and walked back over to Joe shaking her head.

"This guy just won't give up. I don't get it. Why is he so obsessed with me?"

Joe looked at her "Well look at you. You're hot." And hugged her.

Joe said, "Let's go get changed and grab some lunch."

As they went upstairs to get changed, Joe grabbed Laura and helped her with her bikini. He started kissing her and backed her up to the bed and laid her down. He pulled off his swim trunks and stood over her playing with her between her legs moving his fingers inside of her while licking her nipples. She moaned with pleasure and then he gently slid himself inside her and pulled her closer to the edge of the bed so he could move deeper inside her and as he did, he grabbed her breasts and played with her hard nipples until Laura said,

"Come with me" and that was it for him. He started to speed it up, faster and harder and watched her beautiful breasts and when he looked her in the eyes he saw a fiery passion and it wasn't long before they were both screaming out with complete and utter pleasure.

They laid there for a while just holding each other and appreciating the fact that they had once again, been reunited and get a second chance at true love and friendship.

Laura broke the silence, "I just want you to know that this whole divorce and alimony thing is going to be very messy and out right, gloves are off, take it to the knock out round type of divorce. Especially with this little twit girlfriend he apparently has now and I don't know how all this is going to come into play but it will be very interesting to say the least."

Joe stroked her hair, "Well, I'll just be the one behind you telling you to get up and keep fighting. I'll be here for you no matter what."

Laura kissed him, "Thanks for that. Now let's go eat. I'm starving."

He joked with her, "I totally forgot you weren't the cuddling kind."

"I don't have time to cuddle."

They splurged. They grabbed some sandwiches and iced teas and they sat out on the deck. They laughed and just loved being together. Laura looked at him and said, "Well, tonight I'm taking you to a place down the road called Jaspers. So we can have a romantic evening without being spied on."

"Oh, Yes. How about our buddy Kev? Should we invite him along?"

Laura gave Joe a dirty look, "Don't you even dare. It's just me and you tonight because you have to leave tomorrow."

Joe saw the sadness in her face and kissed her on the forehead, "Well, let's not talk about that right now and enjoy the time we have."

They showered and got dressed in their best and went and had a romantic dinner at Jaspers Restaurant. It was the best evening Laura had ever had. The rest of the weekend was just as magical and then Sunday morning came along and the tone changed very quickly.

"Unfortunately, I'll have to head back home around three" Joe said. I want to know when I'll see you again before I go."

She smiled at him, "Well, since you have your daughter next weekend, would you mind me meeting her? I can either go there or you both can come here."

"Why don't you come to my house? I don't want to freak Jennifer out by taking our daughter to a girlfriend's home." Laura picked up on the "girlfriend" and didn't know what she thought of that. So, they got dressed and as they started down the stairs to the beach, Kevin appeared.

"Hey, Laura. Can I talk to you for a minute?" Laura walked over to him.

Hi Kevin. How are you?"

He looked at Joe and then at her, "Why are you blowing me off?"

"Kevin, I'm not blowing you off. It's a lot more complicated than what you see or think. I'm sorry if you think I've done something to you. Can we talk about it this evening?"

He started to walk away, "Yeah sure…………..I'll be home."

CHAPTER SEVEN

Kevin was making her uncomfortable.   She walked back to Joe, "What is that guy's problem?"

 She shrugged her shoulders, "I don't know. He's starting to scare me though."

As they walked he asked her, "So, what's going to happen when you have to get back to your life? I can't move because of Genevieve."

"Well, I'm not sure yet. I don't even have a place to live in New York at this point. Legally, the house is mine too but seriously, I don't want it."

Joe looked at her, "Why? If I were you, I'd take the house."

She shook her head, "It's too cold and unfeeling in there. I feel like some places have their own personality and this is not the house for me. It never was. I was never allowed to decorate it the way I wanted to."

Before Joe left for home, they decided that Laura would head to the mountains on Saturday to meet Genevieve. Laura was so excited. She wanted a baby in the worst way and even if something did come about her and Joe's relationship, she didn't like the idea of sharing a child. It made her feel like she would just be looked at as a fill in. But she could at least enjoy the three year old for a while. She knew she was going to stop by the store and get her a million different toys. She knew that Joe probably just pulled in a median income and with child support was probably bringing home just enough to cover a mortgage payment and food.

After Joe left, she figured she would have to talk to Kevin to straighten everything out. She saw him walk down to the beach as Joe pulled out. She strolled over to him. "You want to take a walk?"

He nodded, "Yeah, sure". He continued, "So, you leave to go hiking with a group of people and end up meeting an old boyfriend?"

"Geez Kevin. I weirdly enough ran into Joe who I almost married but because of an unfortunate misunderstanding, we went our separate ways and never spoke to each other again. You have to understand, we lived together for two years and we were very close until he got scared off and never communicated with me what was going on in his head. So, when he begged for me to forgive him and come back to him, I was afraid he would do it again and decided to go our separate ways. We were soul mates through and through."

And Kevin stopped and looked at Laura. "So, you basically are telling me to get lost? That you have moved on? You are something else Laura. I poured my feelings out to you and this is how you treat me? You are no better than your husband." And Laura slapped him.

"I'm leaving." And she started walking away.

The next morning, she called Adam first thing. "Adam, I just wanted to tell you that Edward contacted me Friday furious that all of his accounts were frozen. He told me he would pay me twenty five million to call off the lawyers."

Adam replied, "Oh really? I'm sure the attorneys will want to hear that tidbit of information. Plus, as you know, it's not because of the divorce that everything is frozen."

"Yes, I do know and I'm sure Edward knows now as well as he hasn't called me back. I didn't want to be the one to tell him. I did tell him I knew about Brandi right before I hung up."

"Well, you need to call Jack today to give him a heads up. And seriously Laura, you'll end up with way more than twenty five million."

"Well, that's great. Then I can move here permanently."

Adam asked, "What? Why?"

"Well, it's very strange but I bumped into Joe. Remember Joe? He was right before I started dating Edward? He is divorced and has a three year old daughter that I'm actually meeting on Saturday. I spent last Saturday with him as well. It's the same."

Adam cleared his throat, "Well, that certainly is weird that you would just happen to run into him. What are the chances?"

"Okay, Adam, I need to get back to work on this campaign. It's going very well and I'll let you have a look as soon as I'm done."

"Okay, Laura. You're my number one. Other than that, you are okay there?"

"Yep. It's great".

She was still furious about what Kevin said to her. She felt bad but she found what she lost and was given a second chance to be with someone she has thought of for years. She went through the same routine with her cup of coffee a run and back to her work. But as she sat there working on this campaign, she realized that Kevin never wanted to open up about his past. *I wonder what happened to him. He seems like a lost soul. Maybe I should be a little more understanding. I'll go over and bring him a peace offering and apologize.* So after she was done with her days work, she ran out to grab some soups and salads and brought them back and knocked on Kevin's door. He looked like hell. "Are you okay? I brought us some food so we can eat and discuss what happened. I want to apologize Kevin." He opened the door and let her in with very few words said.

They sat down and she pulled everything out. "Listen Kevin, I'm really sorry that the two days we spent together meant that much to you. You have to understand, I haven't had someone interested in me in the past five years. So, when you started telling me things that I've never heard from my husband, it was flattering and very tempting. And of course the sex."

Kevin looked at her trying to decide what to say to her. "It's my fault. I have never felt this way towards anyone. I had some horrific things happen and I didn't think I would be able to cope with the normal again." Laura waited. She didn't want to spook him if he was about to tell her what the underlying issue really was. "I watched my parents as they were murdered. It was six years ago. It was a robbery that went very wrong. There was nothing I could do to stop it. I'm not sure why they spared my life but it has haunted me as these people were never caught. I wonder every day if they will come after me."

There were tears in Laura's eyes. She went over to hug him. "Oh Kevin, I am so sorry. That is so tragic." He pulled her onto his lap and looked into her brown eyes. "I do love you."

She shook her head, "No. I think you are just in love with the sex." Kevin sighed as she moved off of his lap and into her chair.

"It's more than sex Laura."

"You have only known me for what? A couple of weeks? How can you love someone that quickly?"

"Well, when you have waited six years for someone to pull you out of a state of despair after many women could not, you know that the chemistry is strong."

"Okay, okay. I guess maybe I have to slow down myself and figure things out. It's been five years for me so all this is becoming confusing. Let's just eat and maybe go out for a little while so we are not tempted" Laura suggested.

After they were done, they both went their separate ways to get changed for the outing. They were heading down the beach to a reggae bar/lounge. Laura threw on a white pair of capris with a low cut and fitted purple tank top. She added a long necklace to her ensemble with a squirt of her Prada perfume. She grabbed her shoes and walked over to Kevin's. He looked great. He was wearing white cargo shorts with a button down short sleeve black shirt. Of course he always wore a gold necklace which looked really good against his black shirt. He left a couple of the buttons undone. He hugged her, "You look phenomenal. And you smell so good."

She giggled, "Thanks, you look pretty good yourself." So, they walked down the beach until they reached Reggie's Reggae bar and lounge. They took a seat at the open bar.

Kevin ordered for them. A couple of margaritas. Kevin spotted a couple of his friends. "Let me introduce you to some of my friends. Jonah, Jose`, and Krista, this is Laura."

"Very nice to meet some of Kevin's friends."

Jonah joked, "It's very nice to meet a woman who has brought Kevin out of isolation." And they all laughed. As they sat there and mingled, Laura started to feel sorry for Kevin. It seemed as if his friends had little respect for him. They were telling her they'd been friends for the last ten years but something didn't seem right to her. She tried to stick up for Kevin while she was there. She was starting to get a little protective.

It started to get late and Laura was starting to feel the alcohol and knew she needed to go home and to bed so she could function in the morning. She had to touch base with Adam as well. As her and Kevin walked back, her phone rang. She looked and it was Joe.

"Who is it?" Kevin asked.

"It's Joe. I'll talk to him tomorrow."

"Listen Laura, I'm not making you choose but if you have your mind made up to take on this guy, I will be crushed." She put her arms around him and kissed him. He pushed her down in the sand and started getting a little too aggressive for her. He went up her shirt and she knew this was not the right thing to do.

"No, Kevin. I don't feel like this is the right thing to do right now."

He stopped and sighed, "Please just let me pleasure you. No sex, I promise."

"Not here. Let's go back to your house."

She knew that she was in a very tough situation and she started thinking to herself,

"How in the hell did I get myself into this? How do I get myself out? Go back to New York?" As they walked into his house he picked her up and carried her to his bedroom. "Please Kevin. I have to get up in the morning. I thought we decided to take it slower."

"I know. I can't help it. You do this to me. Please, just tonight." So as he pulled her pants off and almost ripped her top off, he started to feel her body. "I promise, no sex. Just pleasure." And he pulled her panties off and started to explore her with his tongue and fingers. He was so turned on at that moment. He wanted to take her right then but was trying to show her how much he cared for her. He made her come six times and then moved up to kiss her stomach and neck hoping she would change her mind and let him have her. She grabbed him and stroked it until he came on her breasts. But he wanted so much more. He kissed her passionately, "You are truly a drug to me. I am an addict now and I'm hooked."

"I really have to go. It's really late and if I stay here, I know what will happen." He grabbed his boxer briefs which looked amazing on him.

"You have such little faith in me. I told you that there would be no sex tonight."

She shook her head, "Yes, I know but this is getting out of hand. It's making everything so much more confusing. I can't think straight when you keep advancing on me like this."

"Well, I'm sorry. I don't want to make things more complicated for you, really. I am having my party on Saturday and I want you to meet more of my friends."

"Oh, I forgot about that."

He looked at her, "What do you mean?"

She apologetically said, "I'm supposed to meet Joe's three year old daughter on Saturday." Kevin was furious.

"Okay. You can go now. I'm a little upset and want you out. I guess I know where I stand."

Laura was livid. She grabbed her things and ran back to her house. She again, made sure everything was locked tight and went to bed.

CHAPTER EIGHT

As the week went on, she hadn't seen or heard from Kevin. *He must really be upset with me*, she thought to herself. She had been in contact with Joe every day talking about Saturday and what they were going to do with Genevieve. Laura had actually gone out and bought some outfits for her and a ton of different toys. She couldn't wait to show them all to her. She had told Joe how much fun she had buying all of it. And when Friday afternoon hit, she got a text on her phone,

"Can you come over for a minute? I have something for you."

It was from Kevin. *That's weird that he sent me a text*.

Her response back was, "Sure, I'll be right over."

Something in her gut told her there was something fishy going on but she ignored it. When she got there, he had flowers and presented her with a beautiful necklace with an emerald and chocolate diamond pendent. "Laura, these are to show you how truly sorry I am for what I've said and what I've done to you."

"Kevin, this is way too much. You really didn't need to buy me these things"

He looked at her, "I would really like you to come over tomorrow for the party."

"I already told you that I have plans. I have toys and clothes galore for little Genevieve."

"Listen Laura, if that's all you are looking for is a baby, I will give you a baby." And he came closer, grabbed her and kissed her.

"Kevin, it's not just that. I hardly even know you. You hardly know me. And your behavior is starting to worry me."

"What behavior is that?" as he backed off to look at her face, he then added, "I'm just trying to give you what your husband never did."

"And I appreciate that. I do. I really like you but let's just cool it down a little and see what happens. I am going back over to my place to relax. Thank you so much for the flowers but I can NOT accept this necklace."

He looked at it, "Well, I have no one else to give it to and I selected it with you in mind so you have to accept it."

"Kevin really. It looks very expensive. Can't you take it back?"

He smiled and simply said, "No."

"Well, thank you. It's gorgeous."

"Can I at least join you for a little while? I just made a kick ass salad and have no one to share it with."

Laura looked at his sweet face, "Sure, come on over."

As they ate, Kevin wanted to know more about her family. He was an only child and didn't know what it was like to have a big family. After his parents passed away, no one in his family spoke any more. It tore everyone apart. Laura said, "I figured something as tragic as that would bring everyone closer."

"Well, they pointed their fingers at me. They thought I killed them for their money." Laura was afraid to pursue this conversation any further. She didn't know why.

"Well, certainly, they had to have an investigation on the incident to show that you were not at fault….right?"

"Oh……yeah. The investigation was not conclusive. There was nothing tying anything to the killers. I saw two guys with masks on. They beat me up pretty bad after I found my parents dead. Again, I don't know why they didn't just shoot me too. They found jewelry missing as my mom and dad had insurance out on most of the high end stuff and they ripped everything apart looking for cash. I think they got away with $100K that was hidden in one of the desk drawers in the office which is usually locked.   So, whoever it was must have found the key or the drawer was unlocked.   I knew my parents kept money in there. They did for years. They should have never kept that much cash in the house but they were old school and paid everything in cash."

"That is just horrible, Kevin."

"It has been really tough trying to forget what I had seen. I am still angry knowing that these guys are still out there somewhere. I always wonder if they'll come after me." Now she just felt awful for how she was treating him.

"Well, listen. After I get back from Joe's, I'm more than likely going back to New York for a week or so to meet with the divorce attorney and get all that straightened out, I promise I will meet all of your friends. I just have to be honest with you. The friends I met the other night, Jose` and Jonah……….I wasn't too fond of them."

"Really? We've been great friends for years. Trevor and I have only been friends for the past five but he's a good guy."

She looked at him, "I just don't feel like they respect you. I was sticking up for you at the reggae bar the other night. Their comments were excessive and very unnecessary."

"Oh, they just kid around a lot. It's all in fun." So she dropped it.

So they talked late into the night. He never pressured her or laid a hand on her to make any kind of sexual advance which she thought it to be weird. But that was fine with her. She needed to figure out what she wanted for once. And as much as she wanted Kevin every time she saw him, she knew it was making him think that she was his exclusively.

He looked at her and kissed her cheek, "I will let you get to bed" and he smiled, "by yourself, if it has to be that way and I guess I'll see you when you get back. I would say have fun but I would rather have you here spending time and having fun with me."

"I know. I'm sorry. I didn't know I would run into an ex-boyfriend while I was here. I really am just anxious to meet his daughter."

Kevin looked into the glass doors and said, "Yes, I see" and pointed to all the stuff. "How do you think you are fitting all that into your car?"

Laura laughed, "I don't know."

The next morning, Laura got up and was so excited. She crammed every last thing into her car. She looked at Kevin's house and all of sudden she saw him walk down to meet her. "Wow, I see you have done the impossible." They both laughed. He grabbed her and kissed her so long and deep, it made her yearn for him. Still holding her, he looked at her and said, "I thought about you all night. What will it take for me to show you that I am very serious about you? I want you to myself. I know you think you have other plans with this guy but I truly would make you a happy wife AND a mother."

Laura knew she was in trouble. "I'm not sure Kevin. I really like you but I'm not sure if it's just sexual."

He smiled, "So you do like making love to me. I knew it." Kevin let her go. "Okay. Do what you need to do but make sure you think about me often."

Laura smiled and said, "I will."

As she drove, she was thinking about Kevin's behavior. "He went from aggressive to possessive to almost too nice." Laura thought. *Maybe he has been alone for so long, he doesn't know how to act?* She stopped trying to figure it out and thought of all the toys in her car. It made her laugh. When she pulled into Joe's driveway, he walked out with little Genevieve. She had pony tails in her hair and she was adorable. Laura got out and gave Joe a big hug. He picked up Genevieve and Laura looked at her and said, "I have some things for you." Laura opened the trunk and pulled bag after bag after bag. Genevieve's eyes lit up. One of the toys was a little pink tricycle. She was having a hard time using the pedals so while Joe took everything in the house, Laura worked with her on that.

When everything was in the house, Joe came back out and gave Laura the biggest hug and kiss. "What did you do? Buy the whole store? You did way too much."

Laura smiled, "But it's for her." She went over to Genevieve, "Do you want to see what else you got? I bought you a doll and a doll stroller and a doggie that walks and barks and tons of clothes." So, they went inside so that they could open boxes and put together some of the toys and accessories.

Joe looked at her, "Thanks for this. We'll be here all day trying to get these toys out and putting them together."

"Well, we'll do a few now and a few later. Is there a park we can take Genevieve to play?

We can let her play with some of her toys first. Let's put some of these together for her and then I want to take you both out for dinner as well."

Joe looked at her, "Why are you doing all this?"

"Well, I may be going back to the city next week so I want to go all out this weekend."

"Oh" is all Joe said. He looked so disappointed.

"I'm sure it won't take me long to get everything straightened out and then I can come back."

As the day went on, Laura had so much fun with Joe and Genevieve but she started to see where things could get dicey. She thought to herself, *how are Joe and I supposed to bond when he already has a life started without me?* When they had a full day at the park and then dinner out, Genevieve fell asleep in her car seat. Laura said, "Thank you so much for sharing your daughter with me today. She is a little love. But I can see where this could get complicated between you and I. You already have a life started without me and I feel like I'm intruding."

"No. No Laura. You are not intruding. Why would it get complicated? I told you that Jennifer and I get along great and if anything ever came up, we both are willing to step in for each other." Joe grabbed Laura's hand and kissed it. "I promise it would not ever get complicated between us."

Laura looked at him with concern in her eyes, "It should've been us in the first place."

When they got back to Joe's house, he pulled little Genevieve out of her car seat and carried her into the house. By the time they got in the house she was awake and ready to start playing with her new toys. "Listen, could I help you with her bath and with getting her to bed? Then I'll take off after that."

"Sure" Joe said. "Come on Genevieve, let's get you in the bath tub with these new bubbles that Laura got you."

"Princess bubbles", Laura added in. So, Laura drew her bath and made sure there were enough bubbles in there for her. While Joe washed her, Laura grabbed the new pajamas that she bought for her along with her very own hooded bath towel. The hood was of a butterfly with antennae.

When Laura brought everything in Joe looked, "Wow, you really thought of everything didn't you" and he shook his head. Laura knelt down to play in the bubbles with Genevieve. "You are too much Laura", and Joe kissed her.

After bath time was over, while Joe got Genevieve in her pajamas, Laura started to pick up all of the toys that were scattered and she tidily placed the ones that were opened in Genevieve's room. The others, she kept in the bags and put them in the living room closet for another day. "You can open those the next time you see her. That way she gets a chance to play with what she has open."

"Thank you so much Laura for everything you did today. Can you stay the night with me?"

Laura looked at Genevieve, "I'm not sure that would be the right thing to do. Do you?"

He grabbed her hand, "Please stay. I don't know when I'll see you again."

She smiled, "Okay.   I guess it would be alright."

"Good. I want to show you how much I appreciate you when Genevieve goes to sleep."

After they read Genevieve a couple of books and tucked her in, they turned on her night light and shut the door. They walked into the living room to find something on television until they knew she was definitely asleep. They found they didn't watch much of the television. They were all over each other. Joe did not want to wait. "Let's move into the bedroom."

He closed the door and locked it, came over to Laura and slowly undressed her and then himself. They fell into bed both completely naked and he made sure there was not one inch that he had not touched or found with his tongue. He was completely into her and was more worried about satisfying her then himself. He went down on her and could not give her enough. She was trying to be quiet but as she came she gasped. She pulled him up to her and he was so hard. She stroked him and he couldn't wait any longer. "I want you so bad Laura." He had a built in headboard with shelves and mirrors. When he turned her over on all fours, he could see her full breasts moving each time he plunged himself inside her. It didn't take him long to climax. He grabbed onto her hips and you could hear the slapping of his upper thighs into her and it got quicker and quicker and then finished as he took the final plunge and moaned as quietly as he could.

"I'm not done with you." He started kissing her all over again. He loved her breasts. He started getting hard again and pulled her on top of him. "I want you to come on me." As she rode him, he kissed and fondled her breasts. "I love your breasts. I want to come all over them." She was so turned on she came. She tried to be as quiet as possible. It was ecstasy. She could not get enough of him. She wanted and she kept taking. She had been without for so long it was her turn to greedily take what she felt she deserved. With

114

that she came again and climaxed one more time when he flipped her over in the missionary position and it was only a matter of seconds and he quietly said, "Oh god" and he finished.

They lay there out of breath side by side. "Wow that was unbelievable." Joe whispered. "You are awesome" He added. "I can't let you leave now. I want more of that."

"Well, you can only have me until morning." She said as she grabbed for the tissue. They fell asleep for a few hours until Joe woke up panicked about the time. He knew he didn't have much time with Laura so he started to move his hands and lips over her still naked body. She awoke with his tongue and fingers inside her and he knew just what to do. He played with her and teased her until she finally moaned and grabbed his shoulders almost digging in her nails as she came. "Oh yeah, that is a great wake up call." And he was already hard as a rock. He slid it in and did her hard and fast until he climaxed and she happily let him. "Is it my turn?" she asked teasingly.

"I'm sorry. I got too aroused too quickly. It's never that I end up waking up to a totally beautiful, naked woman beside me."

They looked at the clock, it read six o'clock. "We should probably get dressed before your daughter gets up."

"Yes, that would be a good idea", Joe agreed. "I wish you could stay with me one more day."

"I will let you know what is going on Monday. But in the meantime, I will go home and start packing up a little just in case. I will be back. I promise". And she gave him a long kiss.

"Well, at least stay for breakfast with Genevieve and I, and then I guess I'll let you go." He smiled at her and it made her so wanted and loved. For once she felt that she actually meant something to someone. It made her the happiest she has ever been.

Sure enough, Genevieve woke up around six thirty. She brought in the baby doll and the super soft teddy bear that Laura had gotten her. "Good morning Genevieve. Can I have a hug?" How did your baby sleep last night? Can I give Teddy bear a hug too?" Joe just watched Laura interact with Genevieve and he smiled as he made scrambled eggs and bacon for everyone. She walked into the kitchen to give her dad a big hug and he picked her up and kissed her.

"How are you little lady bug?"

"Good daddy".

"Do you want me to turn on some cartoons for you?" And Genevieve nodded. So, he walked her into the living room and turned Disney on for her.

After they ate breakfast, Laura gave everyone hugs and kisses and headed for home, well, her temporary home. And of course, it was hard to leave. They had so much fun the three of them.

CHAPTER NINE

When she got home, Kevin was on the beach. She walked out there to talk to him. "Hi Kevin. How are you?"

"Well, better now that your back. How did it go? Did the little one get to play with everything yesterday?"

Laura laughed, "Actually no. There is more to getting those toys out than I remember. It took more time to get them out of the packaging than to put them together. Are you okay?"

"Well, I have to be. I have no control over who or what you want. I have to deal with it. You will come to your senses at some point." And he smiled at her.

"I will? You know I like you Kevin and she leaned down and gave him a friendly kiss." She took a seat in the sand. "I think I have to go back to New York this week. Hopefully, the attorneys took Edward's twenty five million dollar plea and doubled that amount. He was able to pay for his girlfriend's way and padded her account so I should get much more for being his wife."

Kevin grabbed her hand, "It will all work in your favor. This whole thing will pass and you will be able to move on and be able to think more clearly. And hopefully choose me." And Kevin smiled at her teasingly.

When she called the law firm to speak to Jack Larson on Monday morning, his assistant told her to hold that he needed to speak to her right away. So, she was put on hold for a couple of minutes. Jack came on, "Laura, I need you here. Something has happened and the police need you here for questioning."

"Questioning for what?"

"For Brandi's death."

"Is this a joke? This is not funny. What is going on?"

"Laura, she was found dead in her penthouse Saturday night."

"But how? What happened?" She was hung from the staircase chandelier."

"Oh my god……………I'm going to be sick. I'll get there as soon as I can." And as soon as she got off the phone she ran into the bathroom and got sick to her stomach.

She called Joe while he was at work, "What happened Laura?"

"They found Edward's girlfriend dead Saturday night."

"They need me there for questioning. They found her hanging from the chandelier."

"Shit, do they have any ideas who would have done that?"

"I guess not."

Joe was firm, "I'm going with you as a friend. You need someone there for support."

"I appreciate what you are saying but I'm not sure that would be a great move. I don't even know where I'll be staying at this point. I will call you as soon as I get to New York and let you know what my plans are. I am in shock right now."

"Okay Laura. Please be careful."

"I will."

She ran over to Kevin's house. "Kevin!" she was shouting. She was pounding on his door. He opened it and saw the look of panic on her face. "What is going on? What happened?"

"They found Edward's girlfriend dead in her home. They found her hung from the chandelier. I don't know what I'm doing. I have to go back for questioning."

"Laura, look at me. Look at me." And she looked at him.

"I will go over with you to help you pack and I will take you to the airport because frankly, you are in no state to drive yourself. Let's go." And she followed him over. Kevin helped her get everything together and get everything into the car.

"Do you want me to go to New York with you? Are you going to be okay on your own because you don't seem like it."

"I'll be okay. I think. I'm not sure." She felt sick again and ran over to behind the house and got sick to her stomach.

"God Laura. You are NOT okay. You need to calm down" And he walked over and rubbed her back.

"No. I'm okay. I'm alright now."

"Listen Laura, I will go over and pack a small bag just in case you decide to take me with you. I can call my friends to let them know what is going on and to check in on the restaurant and my home."

As Kevin drove them to the airport, he called some of his friends to see if they could help him out for a few days. Apparently, by the sound of the conversation, he must have caught them at a bad time.

They told him they were busy and they would call him back when they had more time. After he hung up he looked confused, "That was really weird. I don't even know what that was all about." But he brushed it off. She didn't need Kevin with her anyhow. It would just make things much more difficult.

She flew back and was in touch with Adam while in travel. She met him at the office and he took her into the police station for questioning. Her attorneys were there as well. She told them everything. About being with Joe Saturday night in California. She showed them her plane tickets and whatever else she thought would help. So, everything checked out and she was off the hook. They had spoken to Edward about it and he was cleared. And he was very upset because Brandi was pregnant with his child. That struck Laura in the gut hard.

"What??? She was pregnant? He told me he never wanted kids. He despises children. You need to talk to him again. *He was upset?* But he didn't want *children with me?* She thought to herself. I can tell you he would be your main person. And because he gave her so much money, he had a big part in her life especially with her pregnant. Tell them Jack."

Jack commented, "Yes, everything is being brought to the table and things came out that we feel may be incriminating against Edward."

"There is just one more thing you should know….There was a letter left stapled to her" the officer said.

"What? What did it say?"

Adam looked at her and said, "That Edward was the one they wanted and he'll be next."

"Oh my god. Does that mean I'm in danger as well?"

"We are not sure about that yet but you and I will talk about it in my office. Are you done with my client officers?" Jack asked.

"Yes, I believe we are."

As Laura, Jack and Adam headed back to Jack's office, Jack mentioned that Brandi was not very quiet with anything. They had interviewed her friends and she told them how she and Edward got into an argument over the baby thing and she wanted him to change his will to leave her everything and to push you out of all of it."

"Really? Boy she is a little conniving bitch isn't she".

"Well, apparently, Edward had a change of heart or something because he told her he would not do that. And soon after that conversation, we find her dead.

Brandi had taken her anger to social media and blasted Edward's name all over it. Apparently, she was trying to start her career in modeling and then after finding out she was pregnant, panicked and she blamed it on Edward for ruining her chances of becoming a model. Now it's just trying to track down the person or persons who did do it. We are still looking at possible suspects.

Adam, I don't have a place to stay yet. And I'm not sure I am ready to be alone right at this moment."

"Well, I thought that was a given, that you were stay with us. How are you feeling kiddo?"

"Seriously Adam, I know this sounds selfish but I just want to take whatever is coming to me and find a place of solitude and spend it with Joe and his beautiful daughter. He is barely getting by on his salary and he deserves so much more.

"Well, let's go back to the office."

For the next week, investigators and police spoke to Laura several times. She knew how it looked but she was not even in close proximity nor would she ever think about doing something so unspeakable. She actually went to her parents for the weekend to just settle down. Of course everyone that was tied to her or Edward was questioned so that meant her whole family. But because of certain similarities at the crime scene as they saw with Edward's father, they knew they were looking for killers who knew what they were doing and had made it their profession. And now, because no one knew who they were going after next, Laura and Edward had security on them everywhere they went.

As the police and FBI tried to tie all these high profile deaths together, they pulled out all files and made it priority number one. Trying to link these killings; two in New York and one in Chicago all between a five year span was near impossible. Whoever did this left no incriminating evidence behind which made the police wondering if the killer was still in the city watching and waiting. There was a murder in Chicago five years ago that fit the same method of operation which involved a Charles Jackson who was a very sought after investment broker as well. So, the fact that all these people except for Brandi were investors in some way, was one part of the story.

Laura and everyone close to her were shook up about the whole terrifying situation and afraid for her as well.

Apparently, in all of these murders, the crooks were able to get away with a substantial amount of money along with a significant amount of high quality jewelry. They were skilled at what they did and made sure they strategically planned well for each raid.

Laura's attorneys contacted her and wanted to sit down with her regarding the divorce. She drove in to their office with security in tow. "Laura, we know there is a lot going on right now but we figured that we could at least get this divorce finalized before a judge so that you could go back to California as that may be a safer place for you right now."

"I'm not sure I would feel comfortable going back and risking someone following me. Especially to Joe's home. He has a three year old daughter that I would not want to put in jeopardy. I'm just not sure where I can go except to a hotel and I don't feel comfortable being by myself."

Jack said to her, "Why don't you stay with your parents upstate just in case there is more questioning. We will make sure you and your parents have plenty of surveillance just in case. In the meantime, before you head there, let's get this divorce going. We did pull up some accounts that Edward had been hiding but other than that, he is clean. We figure, the judge will award you half and that comes in at about one hundred million."

Laura looked at Jack, "Are you kidding? I had no idea that Edward had stashed away that kind of money."

Jack smiled at her, "Well, don't forget. That penthouse was around twenty million but he didn't care. He just looked at that as an investment and in total, he deposited around ten million into Brandi's account."

They sat down in front of the judge for the preliminary paperwork and the figures came out to be one hundred million so she would have to come back for that. However, the divorce was completed. The house was awarded to Laura and of course, the penthouse awarded to Edward. It was quick and Laura did glance at Edward as he sat with his lawyers. He looked weak and pale as if he hadn't slept or eaten in days. She started to actually feel sorry for him. As they all started to walk out of the courtroom, he quickly looked at her and whispered, "I'm really sorry Laura. I didn't mean for any of this to happen."

All she could say is, "It did happen and I hope you can move on with your life after this."

When she was escorted back to the office, Adam spotted her and waved her in. She walked in and he gave her a hug. "Have a seat. How did everything go in court?"

Laura looked at him and shook her head, "Edward looked rough. I don't think he's slept or eaten anything in days. I felt kind of sorry for him."

Adam squinted his eyes at her, "Good God Laura. He ruined your life and you feel sorry for him? I know. You are so sweet natured like that. But you are taking all this heat from the police and FBI and everyone else breathing down your neck to see if you make a wrong turn."

She shrugged, "Well, they can follow me all they want and ask me questions for months until they find whoever is doing this. I don't care for all of this security being everywhere I am but I know it is necessary. The main thing is, is the divorce is final. The house is mine but not until Edward removes his belongings. So, they gave him one month. I'll probably be selling it anyhow."

"Well, that is the first step. Now you just need his money." And he smiled.

"Jack feels that I should stay with my parents for the time being. They will make sure there is surveillance and we will be well secured there. So, I guess I'll work from there. I have wrapped up the Fine Design account so give me the next big one on your list."

"Oh yes. I forgot to tell you with everything that has been going on that I had several calls and actually met with a brand new clothing line and want you to run with it."

"Okay. What is it?" Adam smiled. It's called Laurel's Lace and Lingerie."

Laura shook her head, "You're kidding? Okay. I will work my magic. So, I guess, I'll grab my stuff from your house and head to my parents this evening." As she got up to walk out of Adam's office he asked, "So, how much are you going to be worth?"

She smirked, "Enough to buy out this company and three others if the numbers were correct."

CHAPTER TEN

As she is followed by undercover agents to her parent's house, she was told that her parent's house was secure. She wanted to give her mom and dad a heads up so they knew what was happening. Laura didn't feel totally protected and didn't want to put her parent's in harm's way but until the FBI could figure it out, she really had no choice in the matter.

She worked from there and spoke to Joe a couple of times. She watched what she said as she knew her phone was tapped. It was really starting to get on her nerves. After a couple of weeks of being with her parent's she let the authorities know that she really wanted to head back to California. As much as she loved her parents, she had had enough of being stuck there. She had spoken to Adam about moving but still working for the company while acting as a consultant and he didn't have a problem with that. She would just meet with him at least once on each account so that they were on the same page and she could go to work on it. Laura was the best at what she did and he really needed her there. She didn't DARE talk to her parents about her possibly moving to California or about Joe. It was too soon. She didn't need that stress right now and it was NOT the right time. She just got divorced. Until she had that money in her account, she wasn't doing anything.

When she flew back out to Adam's beach house, she was told that there would be agents watching her and the house. Laura could not wait until all this was concluded. *Great. I'll be running with people watching me the whole time.* She thought to herself. *Are they going to watch me having sex too? I hate this no privacy.*

As soon as she pulled into the driveway, Kevin came out to see who it was. He ran down the steps to give her a hug and she was actually relieved to see there was no one watching her. Kevin looked at her glancing around with puzzlement on her face. "Laura, what's wrong?"

"Oh nothing. There are supposed to be federal undercover agents watching me while I'm here for my protection and I don't see anyone."

He gave her another hug and a big kiss and said, "Well, maybe they'll be along in while.

God, I missed you so much. I didn't even get a call from you. I had no idea what was going on so I called Adam once to see how you were."

"Well, the divorce is final. I am actually looking for a house here somewhere. Adam agreed to let me work as a consultant but only for our company, Fusion, Inc. She giggled, he has no choice as after my divorce, I can afford to buy out the company and take over."

"Well, let me take you out for a dinner to celebrate at least."

"Okay, but then I have to get up early to see Joe." Laura regretted saying that after she saw the look on Kevin's face.

"So you still have your heart set on this guy", Kevin said.

"I told you Kevin. We just have that connection that we had years ago. I'm not going to apologize for that."

Kevin looked out at the ocean while there was silence between them. And as she looked at him, she wanted to tell him how hot she thought he was but she didn't want to start something.

"Do you still want to go to dinner Kevin?"

"Yeah…..sure."

They both went and got ready to go out and Laura kept looking out the windows for undercover cars but she saw none. It started to make her a little nervous. When Kevin came over to get her, he spotted her looking out every few minutes. "Why are you being so paranoid?"

She looked from the window and to Kevin, "I'm not. I'm just worried. You have no idea what it was like for me in New York. Even my parent's house that was six hours away had surveillance and I was escorted wherever I went. So, when they say there will be agents here, there should be agents here."

Kevin hugged her, "Well, I have you in my sights and nothing will happen."

"No. I know. But I'm going to have to make a call tomorrow about it."

The two of them went out and had a wonderful dinner together. It was the first time she felt normal since she had been in New York. After a couple of glasses of wine, Laura started asking questions about Kevin's parent's deaths. With all the talk about all the people being in high finance she wanted to know more about what his parent's did for a living. "Well, my dad owned the restaurant I have taken over but my mom was an investment broker dealing with wealthy LA clients. They trusted her more than anyone in the industry. So did my dad.

They had some hefty sums invested in stocks and hedge funds and whatever else came their way. She dealt with a couple of great trade platforms that made everyone a lot of money. She had been in the paper on several occasions as my parents made hefty donations to organizations around the area."

She started to feel uneasy, "Okay, so my husband and his father were into the same kind of thing. I would hear them discuss the trades here and there before his dad was killed.   And apparently this Charles Jackson was one them as well."

"Who is Charles Jackson?" Kevin asked her.

"I guess he lived in Chicago and was an investment guru. He made a lot of people, a lot of money and he was murdered in the same way Edward's father was. Now they're after Edward. But that's all I know."

Kevin started getting edgy, "So you are saying that all these murders could be related? How would that be possible? These people are all over the place not just one city. The police and FBI told me that it was a robbery gone wrong."

Laura felt that she needed to change the subject as it was making her feel uncomfortable discussing it as well, "I'm not sure. It's just speculative. I've had a lot of time for my mind to ponder up crazy scenarios."

He smiled, leaned in and kissed her on the cheek, "When criminals catch wind that someone has money, they target them."

Laura smiled, "Yeah, you're right."

When they drove back to the houses, Laura still saw no one watching out. "I just feel like there is something wrong. I don't feel safe."

Kevin grabbed her hand, "Will you stay with me for the night?" Laura thought about it for a minute and looking at Adam's beach house thought it might be a good idea not to be alone seeing there was no one watching out for her.

"Yes, I think that might be a good idea. But no funny business mister." Laura said as she gave him a little shove in the shoulder.

He held up his hands, "I promise no funny business."

So, they entered Kevin's house and settled in on the couch. "Let me get us some water and we can see if I can find a movie on TV. If not, I can order one for us."

"Sounds good to me." Kevin came back in with a couple of glasses and handed one to Laura. "Thanks Kevin."

As they sat there, Kevin started kissing Laura's neck. "Please Kevin, please don't" she said to him as she moved over.

"But why Laura? We are so great together. I am totally into you."

She looked at him, "Kevin, you are only into me on a sexual level. I'm just afraid you are just infatuated with me and that never lasts. I really like you but right now, there is just too much going on. Let's not make it more confusing than it already is."

He sighed, "Okay fine. But you are so wrong."

She firmly said, "I will sleep down here and you will sleep upstairs so there is no temptation. Got it?"

He was like a little kid, "Yeah......I got it."

The next day Laura was going to see Joe. She told him what was going on and that she wanted to see some houses and thought it would be great if he could go with her. After all, she was going to give him the option to give up his job. He didn't realize how much money she was actually getting in the divorce. So, as she pulled up some possible homes that she liked, she looked at Joe, "Do you care if we are two hours away from Genevieve or is that too far? I was looking at some on the coast."

"I'm not sure what Jen would say to that and what about my job? I'm not driving that far for work." Laura smiled as she kept looking and didn't even look at him when she said, "You don't need to work anymore. Find a hobby."

Joe came over to her and looked down at her, "What do you mean? I have to work."

She looked up at him, "Well, I think the one hundred million that I will be getting through the alimony will hold you over."

Joe rubbed his hands over his face, "One hundred million? Are you serious? But Laura, that is your money. I need to keep working."

Laura said, "No, I am going to keep working only because I like what I do and it is my identity. Plus, Adam would kill me if I quit. I just want you to be able to have Genevieve more without worrying about a work schedule. That would help Jennifer out too. So stop and help me look for a house that we will be living in."

Joe shook his head, "I can't take your money Laura. And are you asking me or telling me that I'm moving in with you?"

She smiled and said, "Well, you can help me pick out MY house and if you choose to move in with me then that is your choice. I'm not making you do anything."

And she added in, "It's not all my money. It's my pain and suffering money. We can thank Edward for that." And she smiled at him.

After they had narrowed the search down to about five possible homes, she headed back to the beach house to do some more research on all of them. They had planned on looking at them again with a realtor so they could physically see the inside instead of looking at pictures and driving by. They figured they would do this on Saturday.

As she worked through the week and set up the appointments for Saturday, she and Kevin hung out from time to time but nothing romantic. He had been super sweet. "I'm having a party on Friday evening. I don't care if you bring Joe but I want you there."

Laura made a fruit salad for the party and bought a few bottles of wine to take over. She waited a little while until the party got started and decided to go over. What she witnessed when she walked through the door was not at all what she expected.

She walked in and people were getting a little too comfortable in the living room. She happened to scan the place and people were coming in and out of the bathroom sniffing and rubbing their noses as they came out. She just assumed that what they were doing was not at all legal. She was freaking out inside but didn't want to look like it. She went looking for Kevin but couldn't find him anywhere. She recognized Jonah and asked him if he'd seen Kevin. Jonah just smirked and said, "Yes, he's upstairs." And as she followed the steps up to his room, she noticed Jonah was following her.

As soon as she walked into Kevin's bedroom, she noticed he was tied up on the floor and it looked as if he had been beaten pretty badly. She went to turn to leave to get help and Jonah and Jose grabbed her. Laura tried to fight them off, "I don't know why you are doing this but get off of me!" They laughed while they tied her to the bed.

Jonah looked at her and then at Kevin, "No. I think we'll be on you, you rich bitch." All of a sudden, fear came over her and she realized that something was very wrong. *How do they know I'm rich? Did Kevin tell them something?* she thought to herself.

"Wait! I thought you were Kevin's friends. Why are you doing this to him?" Laura said trying not to sound too panicked.

Jonah started laughing, "Oh yeah. He is a friend. In fact, his parents were just the first of our payday."

Jose looked at Kevin, "we'll kill you just like we did your parents and this time, there will be so many fucked up people here, no one will know anything. We want our share from this bitch first."

Jonah saw the look of shock on her face, "What? You don't think we know who you and your husband are? We've been following Eddie boy for a while. We wanted to give him a chance to get over his father's death before we went after him. But things went wrong and we ended up taking care of his little side kick. Unfortunately, we only got a few pieces of jewelry from her but we figured we would make it up."

Laura looked into Kevin's eyes and saw the apologetic look and horror and he could barely get the words out, "I'm so sorry."

"What in the hell is wrong with you?" Laura screamed at Jonah. "Please let me go and I won't tell a soul. But if you keep me here and hurt me, I swear to you, you will spend the rest of your life in jail."

"Laura, you know I would never hurt you but I'm sure my buddy Kevin wouldn't mind watching me pleasure you."

"You ARE hurting me!"

"Well, let's see if I can help you relax." Jonah said. And he smacked her so hard she was knocked out.

Kevin hoarsely yelled, "NO!" and Jose kicked him so hard in the side, Kevin grabbed his ribs writhing in pain. And to add to the torture, Jonah decided to strip Laura down while she was out cold just to make her feel vulnerable.

When she awoke to find that she was naked, she was horrified and knew what was coming next. She looked at Kevin.

"Kevin, they are going to kill us. How are we going to get out of this?" and she sobbed.

And then she heard them coming up the stairs laughing as if this was all a big fucking joke to them.

Jonah spoke, "Oh, I see the princess has awakened. Does she need a real lover?"

Laura got angry, "Don't you even think about it you piece of shit." Jonah looked over at Jose, "Can I have your belt?"

Kevin pleaded, "Jonah, please don't."

He looked at Kevin, "Haven't you had enough?"

And just then he whipped her twice across the stomach and she screamed and moved and he got her across the hip and part of the buttock. She didn't say another word. Tears were streaming down her face from the pain.

Jonah handed back the belt to Jose. "Let that be a lesson to you bitch."

And they both walked back down the stairs.

Kevin was crying for her. "Laura, I'm so sorry. Are you okay?"

Through her tears she responded, "I'm in so much pain, I wish they would just kill me now."

And this went on for the next couple of hours as Kevin had to listen and watch in horror and couldn't do anything to save her. The torture that Kevin and Laura endured were unspeakable. She had no idea what they would do to her next. She thought, *are they going to rape me? Will they drug me? Or will they just decide to kill me? Or will I be tortured to death?*

She didn't have her cell phone. She left it next door as she thought she was just coming over for a few minutes. Joe started calling her cell phone when she didn't show up. He thought she must have blown him off which didn't seem like something Laura would do.

Joe kept calling and was getting worried when she didn't call him back or return any of his texts. He called his sister Joanna to see if she could take Genevieve for dinner. He explained to Joanna what was going on. "Joe, are you sure she was coming? What if you are wasting your time?"

"I just have a weird feeling that something has happened. There was a guy next door that seemed like he wanted to kill me and was very strange. I saw the way he looked at Laura. It was scary."

"Okay. I'll take her but you need to call me if something happens."

As he was on his way to the beach house, he kept trying to call her cell. "Please be okay." He said to himself. He drove as quickly as he could. When he finally got closer, his stomach just told him there was something very wrong. He saw that Kevin's house was full of people. He figured since Kevin knew what he looked like, he would park his car down the road and go into the back entrance of Laura's beach house. The door was unlocked. He walked in and listened, "Laura?" And he didn't see her downstairs but saw her phone sitting next to her computer in the dining room. He looked at her phone and there were all of his messages, not even touched. He ran upstairs, "Laura?" And there was no one upstairs. Her bag was packed on the bed for her trip to meet with him he assumed. "Okay, how do I do this? Do I call the police or do I go over there and find her myself?"

He had a friend, Warren, who was a police officer but not in this jurisdiction. He decided to call him, "Hello".

"Hey Warren, its Joe. I need a favor from you." And he continued to tell him what was going on and his suspicions. "All I'm asking you to do is to come down here with your badge and back me up. I'm going in as soon as I know you are on your way. That way if I get jumped, I'll know someone will be there to drag my ass out."

Warren said, "Okay, give me the address and I'm out the door. It will take me about twenty minutes to get there."

"Okay Warren…thank you."

CHAPTER ELEVEN

As soon as he hung up, he walked over there and cautiously made his way up. No one really noticed him walking in and he didn't see Kevin or Laura. Joe looked around and happened to see some cocaine on one table and he caught a glimpse of an empty syringe left sitting on the counter. There were drugs and needles and alcohol flowing like Niagara Falls. *"Proceed with caution"* is all Joe could think. "I'm looking for Laura or Kevin."

Trevor chimed in drunkenly, "Well buddy, I haven't seen the little bitch or that piece of shit in a while." She's such a fucking tease." Joe was so angry, he wanted to pound that guy right then but felt it better to keep cool.

 "Well, she was supposed to meet me and my daughter and she never showed or even called."

Trevor sneered, "Who knows. She's probably on to the next guy that came along and wanted her pussy."

Joe thought to himself, "*One more comment like that and this guy is going down.*" "It is odd though as I found her cell phone on the dining room table next door and I know she never leaves that behind wherever she goes."

Trevor replied, "Well, did you look upstairs? She's probably boning someone right now. You could probably catch her."

Joe looked at Trevor long and hard, "I don't know who you are but something is wrong and I think she's here. If you don't mind, I would like to look."

Trevor shoved him, "I do mind. She is not here."

Joe started walking towards the stairs, "I want to make sure."

He started taking the stairs four at a time with, Jonah and Jose right behind him and others followed. And Trevor was careful to stay downstairs but he yelled up, "Here comes her boyfriend." Trevor almost acted as the lookout guy. He actually sat out on the deck to make sure it was clear as he knew what was coming. Joe spotted Laura tied up naked on the bed and then Kevin tied up on the floor all beaten and bloody and went wild. He fought so hard but it was only him against six others. He kept it up for a while but just couldn't compete with a bunch of people hopped up on alcohol, cocaine and whatever else was in their system. They just felt no pain with each blow Joe threw but Joe felt every hit and went down hard. Laura watched in terror and humiliation.

Just as Joe laid on the floor bleeding and in pain, Jonah looked at him and said, "Now you can watch me fuck your girl." And then he looked at Laura and now we have an audience" as he glanced at everyone standing there.

 Just as he got on top of her and unzipped his pants, they heard "Police, hands up!" Warren not only showed but he made sure there were locals on the scene as well. Two officers ran upstairs and saw what was happening. One grabbed Jonah and threw him to the ground and the other tended to Laura. There were police surrounding the house so no one could go anywhere. Warren came up and found Joe bloody and beaten pretty bad. He called into his radio. "We need a couple of buses here now. Possible rape victim."

He looked at Joe and asked him, "How did you know? You are one lucky bastard."

Joe looked at Warren, "I need to get over to Laura. Help me over there."

So, Warren grabbed onto Joe and sat him on the bed next to Laura.

"I am so sorry Laura. I wish I could have gotten to you sooner. Did they rape you?"

She looked at him and said, "No. I don't think so. Maybe they did when I was knocked out. I'm just glad you figured something was wrong or I was going to die. Jonah and Jose` admitted to killing Kevin's parents for the money and Edward's father and his girlfriend."

Joe looked at the police, "Did you hear that? They admitted to the killings."

Kevin was in bad shape, physically and mentally. He was crying for Laura. "I am so sorry Laura. There was nothing I could do to save you."

Joe actually felt bad for him, "Kevin, I'm sure that was pure hell having to watch what Laura had to go through and finding out that your friends betrayed you. I'm sorry man."

The ambulances took the three of them away to get checked out. Joe was out the next day but Laura and Kevin were in for a couple of days for further observation. They wanted to make sure she didn't have any infection as the cuts were so severe from being whipped by the belt and with Kevin, they wanted to make sure that there was no internal bleeding from his injuries. Laura was so relieved that Joe was intuitive enough to save her life. She was sure that she would have never gotten out of there alive. Everyone in that house was arrested and questioned and who knows what else. There were drugs all over the place. But Jonah and Jose were arraigned for murder. Jonah had extra charges brought up against him. He was going away for a very long time. But Trevor was questioned and released and in a vulnerable situation right now.

When they got to the hospital, Joe was concerned about Genevieve. He did call his sister to let her know what had happened but told her not to say anything to his ex-wife. "I will be there tomorrow to pick her up." He told her.

After he received his discharge paperwork the next morning, he went in to check on Laura. She gave him the biggest hug. "You have no idea how grateful I am. I don't know how you thought enough to check on me but however this whole thing has come about is something of fate. Things could've gone another way."

He looked at her, "I'm just sorry that I didn't get to you earlier. It makes me cringe to know that you were tortured like that." He was afraid to say it. "And almost raped and murdered." Lucky for her, they performed a rape kit and it showed nothing.

It infuriated him that someone could do that. "Listen, I have to go get Genevieve but I really want to make sure you are okay. I am taking a couple days off because I am hurting pretty good and I don't want you staying in that house. I want you close to me so that I know you are safe."

Laura cried. "Okay. I will head your way once I get out of here tomorrow. I will make sure I call you as well." He gave her a kiss and headed out. He looked back and said, "I will see you later. And if you need me to come get you, let me know."

When Laura was finally discharged, she got a cab back to the beach house. She did not feel comfortable going back. Once the cab dropped her off, Kevin's house was all closed off as it was a crime scene. There were still investigators there. She hurriedly grabbed all her clothes, computer and phone and anything else she had brought with her. She wanted to take a shower but figured she could do that when she got to Joe's. She just wanted out. She made sure the doors were all locked and all the lights off. She looked at her phone and saw that there were tons of calls from Joe on Friday. As she drove up to his house, she put a call into Adam. "Hi Laura, what's up?"

"Well, I have to tell you that I just got out of the hospital."

"Are you okay? What happened?"

"Well, Kevin's friends are psychos. They kidnapped me, tied me up and tortured me." They beat poor Kevin and Joe to a bloody pulp and Kevin has nowhere to stay," She realized she was yelling at him.

"Oh my god! What in the hell? Are you okay? Where are you now?" "Well, I won't stay next to a crime scene so I am on my way to Joe's. He's the one who saved my ass which ended him in the hospital as well. "I am so sorry Laura. What friends?"

"Jonah and Jose`"

Adam couldn't believe it, "Those two did all that? I knew them. But they were all buddies. Why?"

Laura angrily said "Buddies don't kill your parents. They confessed to killing Kevin's parents."

"Poor Kevin. It's bad enough he watches his parents get killed but by his so-called friends?"

"And that's why they were targeting me. They confessed to killing Edward's girlfriend. I guess they will be questioned on some of these other high profile murders as well. They were coming after Edward and myself.   I would be dead right now if it hadn't been for Joe. I have to speak to my investor tomorrow to see if I can get my hands on any of my funds."

"Okay. Just get some rest. That is some ordeal that you have been through. I would feel better if you were here now."

Adam added, "I'll call Kevin and let him know that he can use our home until the investigators are done with his. What a mess."

Once she told Joe she was on her way, he felt relieved.

"Okay. Good. I told Jennifer what happened and she came and took Genevieve. I'm in way too much pain to run after a three year old right now and I'm sure you are as well."

"Unfortunately, our plans didn't work out like they were supposed to. I already called my boss to let him know that I will back in New York within the next few days. I just need to heal a little and go back and take care of the alimony settlement. I want to finalize it and then I want to move out here to be with you. But we'll talk about that later."

"Okay" Joe said smiling. "Please be careful driving."

Once she pulled in his driveway, he came out to help her with her bags but gave her a hug first. "I feel so much better that you are here with me. Safe."

"Yeah, I'm pretty relieved myself." "Let's go in and relax" Joe said.

"Oh yeah………….that sounds great."

So they laid down in bed and slept for hours and it felt so good. They were both in a lot of pain. Joe looked at Laura and said sadly, "I am so sorry he did what he did to you. When I saw you like you were, I wanted to break that guy's neck. You have no idea how much adrenaline was running through my body."

Laura kissed him and reassured him, "The main thing is that I am alive. I thought for sure I was dead after he told me he had killed Kevin's parents and he had been watching Edward and me for a while. I will heal in time. I will not let this scar me because I have too many good things going on in my life. I'm not going to let a one little scum bag ruin that for me. I'll be fine. I promise."

Joe smiled at her, "Well good, because I would love to give you your own baby. Well our own baby. When you're ready."

"That would make me the happiest person in the world. When I'm ready. I do think that we should check on Kevin though. He is staying at Adam's beach house until the investigation is done at his. I think he is going to need a friend right now. Maybe I should've stayed there to help take care of him. He has so many broken bones that he has some pretty heavy medications he is taking. I just want to make sure he is taking them so he's comfortable. Obviously, he has no friends that can check up on him."

Joe looked at her, "Why don't you take a ride down there tomorrow IF you feel up to it. That guy needs to see you because he feels responsible for what happened. I don't think I could handle it if I saw someone physically torturing you without being able to do anything. I know what happened which is bad enough but I didn't see it. So, I think you need to talk to him to reassure him that you are okay."

Laura nodded, "Yeah, I can see that. I'm sure he feels horrible. You should've saw the horror in his eyes. I will never forget the look in his eyes. That poor soul. I will. I'll go speak to him and let him know it is okay. With that said, I'm going to make us some food and we'll take it to the living room?"

"Sounds good to me" Joe agreed as he started to get up slowly out of bed moaning in pain.

Laura grabbed some easy foods to throw together and brought them into the living room. She looked at Joe, "awe sweetie, you look horrible. What are you going to say to your daughter when she asks?"

"I don't know….maybe I fell down?"

After they ate they just relaxed on the couch and watched TV for a while and eventually made their way back to the bedroom. They took care of each other the best they could as they were both in pretty bad shape.

CHAPTER TWELVE

The next morning which was Tuesday, they awoke both feeling a little bit better. To both of their surprise, Joe's sister Joanna stopped over with coffees and breakfast for the both of them. She was very worried as Laura hadn't seen Joanna in a while. She liked Joanna a lot when Joe and she were together years ago but she wasn't sure how Joanna was going to react to her showing back up into Joe's life.

"So how are the patients this morning?" Joanna asked as she started setting out the breakfast for everyone. She looked at Joe and Laura. "Oh, you guys look horrible. I hope those guys are in jail."

Joe replied, "Yeah, they are and they should be dead for what they did to Laura."

Laura shook her head, "Let's not talk about it. It's over and we'll get over it."

But no words needed to be said. Joanna understood fully. "Oh honey. You poor thing."

Laura reassured her, "No, I'm fine. Really."

Joanna waved her hand, "Well, sit down and eat."

"That was really sweet of you Joanna" Laura gestured.

"Well with what you guys went through, I figured you wouldn't feel like cooking."

Joe was in deep thought as he was eating. "You know what Laura? I am going to go with you to talk to Kev. That guy has had it pretty bad and I guess he might need a guy's perspective on this whole situation. And plus, I don't want to let you go by yourself again. Got a gut feeling."

Laura smiled, "Okay, It's just Kevin. But that's fine. He's probably hurting pretty bad himself. I think he got it worse than we did. I think they broke some of his ribs and his arm and he had stitches in his head and his eye brow. I'm not sure what else. I think maybe I'll bring some stuff just in case he needs someone to help him. Even if it's for a couple of days."

When they were done eating, Joanna cleaned up and told them if they needed anything, just to give her a call.

After Joanna left, they showered and got ready to go check on Kevin.

As they started driving towards the beach house, Laura started to feel uneasy. The tension was very prevalent and Joe said something, "Are you okay?"

"Yeah, just thinking of that night is all and I don't want to see that house but I'll be fine. I'm more concerned about Kevin."

As they pulled into the driveway, all the doors were still closed up. Usually by this time, the doors and windows are open to allow the breeze through the house. Joe looked at Laura and asked, "Do you have the keys?"

She dug through her purse and found them, "Yep. Let's go."

As they walked up the deck, Laura unlocked the door and called in, "Kevin?" There was no response. She looked at Joe and shrugged her shoulders. "Maybe he decided to stay somewhere else after all. It doesn't look as if anyone even came in at all. Maybe he's still in the hospital. We'll have to check there I guess."

He said, "I'll just check upstairs real quick." So, as they started up the stairs they started smelling something foul and they covered their noses and looked each other and knew right away there was something wrong.

Joe said, "Maybe you should stay down here Laura and let me go up." She agreed. She just went to the top of the stairs.

Joe went to the double doors that leads into the master bedroom and he peaked in and immediately turned his head and gasped and yelled "Oh God". He pulled his cell phone and called 911. Laura looked at him and started crying, "No…NO! He can't be! Why would he do that? What did he do?" Joe came to her and hugged her.

 "He hung himself. We should've got here yesterday. Damn it!!!"

They went downstairs and waited for the police to arrive and of course Laura felt horrible and she cried hysterically. "He shouldn't have been alone. I should've stayed here with him. He was betrayed by people that he trusted." That's why he did this to himself. I let him down too."

Joe immediately corrected her, "It's not because of you. It's because of Jonah and Jose and all those assholes. Damn!"

Laura was inconsolable. She curled up in a ball on the couch and cried uncontrollably. She hurt all over. Joe sat next to her with his head in his hands as they heard the sirens and it was a moment he would never forget.

Joe spoke to the police and FBI and everyone else on scene. Laura was too upset to talk. It was an eerie and tragic end to a life that had not been lived or a life lived tragically up to that point that could've have had a better life ahead. The lead investigator called Adam to let him know that his house was now a crime scene. He explained to him that he couldn't give him any details at that moment.

Laura looked at Joe, her eyes red and swollen, "I need to call Adam. He is going to be freaking out about all of this not knowing what's going on."

"Why don't you wait until you calm down a little? There is nothing that can be done now."

After they were able to leave, they were both mentally exhausted by what they had just witnessed. Especially, Laura. She just kept thinking to herself that she should have done something different. Her heart ached. She definitely felt something for him but she wasn't sure it was love. Maybe it was. *Oh Kevin. You should still be here.* And she started to cry as she looked out the window in silence.

The whole ride back to Joe's house was quiet. As Joe drove, Laura just thought about all times that she spent with Kevin and how hard he tried to win her over. How romantic he really was. And how sweet and reserved he became in the end. *Why did you do this?* Is all she could think to herself. She was truly heartbroken.

When they got back, Laura just needed some time alone to grieve so she went out back and sat. Joe kept his distance. He understood. He checked in every once in a while. Adam had tried calling her a few times but she didn't answer. She decided to give him a call. "I know Adam."

"Please don't tell me it was Kevin" Adam begged.

"It was Kevin", and Laura started crying and she moved the phone away from her ear.

There was silence and then Adam asked, "What happened?"

Laura composed herself and said, "He hung himself. I can't really talk about it right now. I'm too emotional. I'll be heading back to New York in the next couple of days. My wounds are healing so I should be fine and I'll talk to you then." And she hung up.

She walked back into the house and Joe stood up, "Are you okay?"

"Yes, I'm fine. I do need to go grab my laptop out of my car though and I have my jewelry locked in a small safe that I would like to leave here if that is okay."

He looked at her puzzled, "Well, sure."

"I had to grab all of my expensive jewelry before I left because I was afraid Edward would have taken it all and it's worth a lot and I bought it all myself."

He smiled, "I understand. Bring it in. I will make sure nothing happens to it."

She came back in with her lap top and her jewelry box and handed it to him. "Hide this somewhere safe for me. And in the meantime, I'm going to find myself a flight back to New York so I can finalize everything and move on with my life if I can do that with nothing else tragic happening."

Joe grabbed her and hugged her. "Nothing else is going to happen. I promise. This whole situation was very unfortunate but it would have happened here or in New York. You heard what they said. They were targeting you. You were just in the wrong place at the wrong time."

"I know, how does that happen?"

So she started searching for flights and booked one for the next day.

"Well, I'll be out of your way for a while anyways."

He gently grabbed her face, "I like you in my way" and he kissed her passionately that made her heart start beating faster and her want him badly but she was still so badly bruised and had lashes all over her body that still had to heal.

She looked at him in his beautiful brown eyes, "I want to make love to you right now if I wasn't so cut up."

He felt so bad for her. He saw how bad they lacerated her body. He had been helping her rub cream on the cuts. "I know. You need to heal first. Give it time. We have plenty of time for that." And he kissed her again.

He just melted her heart and made her feel so much better about everything that had happened. He is part of her healing.

She asked him, "Is there any good sushi places around here?"

"Sure. There is a couple."

Laura responded, "Well, I say we go out for a nice sushi dinner and find a movie on TV and get a good night sleep since we have had a very bad day today. I can't say that I won't get emotional here and there but we need to eat."

Laura put on something that was comfortable on her body but dressier and tried to get her puffy, red eyes down but it didn't matter because she just kept breaking down. She decided against the eye make-up. She did what she could with the rest of her face. She didn't really care. She was just grateful to be standing there looking at her reflection.

The dinner was understandably quiet but the food was excellent. Laura was actually relieved to some extent to be going back to New York and working from her office. She wanted the normalcy again. But then she looked over at Joe and felt guilty for having those feelings.

It was an early night for the both of them. Laura cried herself to sleep. She actually slept on the couch. Joe listened to her until he fell asleep and just felt her pain but there was nothing he could do but let her grieve.

The next morning, Laura's phone rang and woke her. She looked and it was Edward. "Yes Edward."

"My God Laura. I heard what happened. Are you okay?"

"I appreciate your concern but I am okay and I'm coming back to New York today. I'm sure you were a little disappointed it wasn't me instead of Brandi but that's the luck of the draw."

Edward was silent. And then Laura thinking about Kevin felt horrible. "I'm sorry Edward.

That wasn't fair of me to say. I am really sorry for your loss."

Edward in a soft tone replied, "Well, if you really mean that, thank you. And I guess I will see you in New York. Will you call me when you get in so we can talk over dinner?"

Laura about fell over. Edward never asked her out to dinner even when they were married. "Sure Edward. I will call you."

She sat there paralyzed as Joe came in the living room and sat down next to her. "Who was that calling so early in the morning?"

"That was Edward."

"What did he want?"

She looked at Joe and said, "He asked me if I was alright and asked me if he could take me to dinner when I get back to New York so that we could talk." She shook her head, "You don't understand. He never took me out to dinner when we were married. So this is a whole different Edward I am getting."

Joe was getting a little nervous and started fidgeting, "Huh, do you think he wants to reconcile? Or something like that?"

Laura made a face, "Oh God no. He already told me he doesn't love me anymore. That pretty much covers it. He probably wants to apologize for cheating and for who knows what else I don't want to hear. OR he is going to try to weasel his way out of paying me my share."

Joe thought about that, "Yeah, probably."

Laura got up and started packing up her things. She looked at Joe, "Remember, there are new toys in the closet for Genevieve when she gets tired of her other ones."

Joe looking distracted replied, "Yes, I remember."

He stopped her from packing and turned her around to face him. "You are coming back aren't you? I just have this feeling you would rather be in New York and there is a chance you may not be back."

"Since I've been here, it's been one thing after another. So out of my norm. We both have experienced some feelings that we can't ignore and we have endured some pretty horrific acts of torture and seeing my friend end his life in such a way...........I need to get back to my office, to my people, to my family and just get back to a normal life again for a while. And when all this settles, I will be back."

The look on Joe's face was frustration and confusion and she didn't know if he was going to cry or scream or throw something or what. All he did was turn around and walk out the door.

She figured she would let him blow off some steam and then she would talk to him. She finished packing and went out to find him. He was chopping wood down behind his house.

She yelled, "Joe....Joe!" He stopped and looked at her with tears in his eyes.

"Go, I have nothing to say to you. I thought we had everything going and this time you are walking away from me. Is this payback from what I did to you eight years ago? Because I already told you I was sorry and that I regretted it."

Laura came closer to him, "No, this has nothing to do with that. I'm not walking away from you. I have work and an alimony hearing pending. I need to get these taken care of. I need to find a home. I'm kind of lost right now Joe."

"You have a home right here."

"Okay, but I still have a job. I have to have some kind of contract put into place through my company stating that I would be a "consultant" through Fusion, Inc. only so that I can work from anywhere. There are a lot of loose ends."

He nodded, "Okay......okay. I understand."

She hugged him, "And why are you chopping wood? Aren't you still in pain?"

"It's not too bad today."

Laura grabbed his hand, "Let's make some eggs and have breakfast before I have to go."

It was a better morning for the both of them. She wished she could make love but her cuts and bruises were still pretty bad.

She smiled at him and said teasingly, "I have to come back to get all my jewelry. I did grab a few pieces to take with me though." One of those pieces was the beautiful pendant necklace that Kevin had given her. She was actually glad she kept it after all.

He grabbed her bags and she grabbed her laptop and they headed for the car. They put everything in and he grabbed her and hugged her. "Please come back to me. I love you."

She looked at him. "You do?"

He nodded, "Yes, I am in love with you Laura Brooks and he kissed her."

"Please call me as soon as you land. And I guess I'll see you when I see you."

She kissed him again, "Give Genevieve a big hug and kiss for me and tell her I'll see her soon."

She got in the car and took off and her heart felt like it had ripped in half. She never said that she loved him back. *It's fine.* She reassured herself.

CHAPTER THIRTEEN

As soon as she returned to New York, she felt renewed. She just escaped the nightmare she was trapped in. Now she just has the marks to remind her of that horrible night. She still thought about Kevin. And knew that that was what she was going to have to discuss with Adam at that moment and she stepped back into Fusion, Inc.

How wonderful to be back in this building again. Her colleagues greeted her and it was refreshing to say the least. She immediately headed for Adam's office.

He saw her coming and waved her in impatiently. He met her at the door and gave her a hug nearly taking her breath away. "Ouch"

Adam let go right away, "Oh, I forgot, I'm sorry. How bad is it?"

"I can show you if you want me to. It's pretty bad. But not as bad as Kevin." And the tears started.

Adam nodded, "Yes, what in the hell happened down there? I send you down to relax and you come back in worse shape than when you left. I need to know what happened to Kev. No one told me any of the details and you were in no shape to talk. Are you okay now?"

"Yeah, I might as well tell you because I feel partly to blame for what happened." And the tears started rolling down her cheeks.

Adam looked confused and handed her the tissue box and told her to sit down. "What do you mean?"

"Kevin came over and introduced himself to me and was really sweet. He made me dinner and everything. No guy has ever been that nice to me in a long time."

Adam knew what was coming next, "Oh………no."

She nodded, "Yes. He seduced me. But then I found out how old he was and I freaked out and I told him that it was over and he said age didn't matter and then I met up with Joe and then Kevin got jealous. But in the end he understood, I thought. And then his friends turned on him and he finds out they killed his parents and they were going to kill him.

Everything just came tumbling down around him including me turning him down and he couldn't handle everything at once."

Adam threw his hands up in the air and said, "It's not your fault Laura. The freakin guy got caught up with the wrong friends. What a shitty way to have the tide turn on you though. Especially a guy who was as nice as they come. Gloria is just grief stricken. You're just lucky you are sitting in front of me right now."

She wiped her face and composed herself. "Yeah, Kevin was super sweet. He kept telling me he was going to win me over some way somehow. He was going to show me how much he loved me." And she covered her face with her hands remembering that day he said it and the intensity and sincerity in his eyes and let the sobs come. She didn't care anymore.

Adam came over to her and rubbed her back while she let it out. "Good God. It got that heated between you two?" And she just nodded her head.

"Oh kiddo...........just let it go. I'm sorry this happened to you."

He walked out his door and told is assistant to grab a cold ice compact and a cold water for Laura.

"Here", he said as he handed Laura the cold bottle of water.

"Thanks Adam."

He asked her, "Okay, what do we need to do first?"

She looked at him with red, teary eyes and said, "I'm going to my office to work on the new account that you gave me." There was silence and then Adam said, "Are you up to working today?"

Laura stood up, "Yes. I'm fine. I'll be fine once I start working. It'll take my mind off everything." And she headed over to her office.

She started working on the new account Laurel's Lace and Lingerie. I guess I'm going to have to call the President of the company, Denise Tempest.

When she was done, she headed back over to Adam's office. She checked to see if he was busy but he waved her in.

He asked her, "When is the court date on the finalization of the alimony settlement?"

"I thought it was this Friday. Let me check my calendar."

Adam looked at her. "Listen, I feel uneasy about something. If it's not this Friday, we are going to talk to the attorney and try and move it up."

Laura laughed, "Yeah right. His attorneys will never agree to that. We'll be lucky if they don't push it back further. Adam? What is wrong with you?"

"I don't know."

"Well, you are starting to freak me out a little bit. Can we talk about where I'm going to be staying until the house is totally mine and the locks can be changed?"

Adam said, "Well, I think you'd be safest staying with our family at the moment until all this blows over and THEN you can do what you want. I thought you wanted to move to California to be with Joe."

"I don't really want to think that far ahead right now. So much has happened way too fast. I need to slow the pace down and think more clearly about what I'm doing. This is MY life."

"I agree with you one hundred percent."

Laura said, "Okay we are totally off subject, I wanted to go over the Laurel's Lace and Lingerie account with you for a minute."

"Sure what do you have?"

So they went over her ideas for about a half an hour and decided to take a break and go out for lunch.

Laura said, "I'll drive. My car has been sitting at the airport for so long it needs to move a little." It was the beginning of October so it was starting to get a little chilly.

As they walked down to the parking lot, she started the car from afar to get it warm and what they witnessed was unbelievable. BOOM!!!! They witnessed an explosion and pieces flying everywhere. They ducked as quickly as they could as they covered their heads from falling debris. They felt the ground tremble and the heat from the explosion while the car alarms were going off everywhere. Cars around hers were damaged beyond recognition while her car was almost non-existent. Adam yelled out, "What the fuck was that? I told you something was wrong!"

Security immediately came running and Laura told them what happened. Police were called to the scene as were FBI and everyone else as it was now a crime investigation. Laura and Adam were questioned by everyone a million times. By the time they were done they decided to order in.

They went upstairs to Adams office and Laura just simply said, "I can't take this anymore. We almost died. Why are people trying to kill me?"

"It's Edward that's trying to kill you."

"Edward doesn't know how to change oil or change a damn tire. He wouldn't know how to plant a bomb."

She calmed down as she recollected her conversation with Edward earlier, "Well, it was strange but Edward called me early this morning wanting to know if he could take me out to dinner so that we could talk."

Adam shook his head and of course waving his hands around, "No way. No way. You are not going to dinner with him. And since when has he ever taken you out to dinner? That is a little strange don't you think? If you do go, there will be some kind of agents following you. I don't trust the man, Laura."

"Yeah, I thought it to be a little strange myself. Maybe he wants to try and persuade me to take less of a cut of his money? Because I know he doesn't want to reconcile. He already told me he doesn't love me anymore so that is basically off the table. I don't know what else there is."

Adam rubbed his chin, "We'll have to talk to the attorneys about this first. We may have to wire you up just in case and someone is going to have to follow you to make sure you're safe. How do you know he doesn't have a contract out on you?"

Laura laughed nervously, "Do you actually think he would do that?"

"Laura, Wake Up! There is what? One hundred million on the table that you are getting from the alimony settlement. Don't you think that that would be worth it to him to hire someone to take you out? Look at what just happened."

"Oh my God…………..What was I thinking? Of course he would do that."

Adam picked up the phone and started dialing. "I'm calling Jack Larson right now. "I need to speak to Jack Larson right away. It's of upmost importance. Yes, it's Adam Grant from Fusion, Inc."

Immediately Jack was on the phone, "Adam, what in the hell happened? You are one lucky bastard."

Adam responded, "I'm assuming your friends at the FBI has started to fill you in on the information because this is serious Jack. I don't know what to do with Laura now. She is in danger. You need to let us know how to proceed. I'm assuming the FBI will let us know what we are to do after they are done downstairs?"

"Of course. They will probably place agents on her now and wherever she goes for a while until they figure out who is out to get her.

And then he opted for the speaker so that Laura would be included in on the conversation.

"Well Jack, I have Laura Jennings here in my office and we may have another little problem."

Jack interrupted, "Laura, with all that you have been through, I hope that you are okay. You have had a horrible ordeal as I have been kept in the loop on everything that has happened and I am so sorry."

She responded, "Well, Thank you but I am healing just fine."

"Sorry Adam go ahead with what it was you were going to say."

"Well, out of the blue, Edward called Laura to ask her to dinner so that they could talk. He never asked her to dinner the four years they were married. Why now? They are not reconciling because he already told her he doesn't love her so don't you find that odd?"

Jack cleared his throat, "Yeah especially hearing his attorneys speaking on his behalf. He doesn't seem like such a nice, honest guy. Seems a little out of sorts to me. I say skip the dinner and save yourself from a possible ambush from whatever he is trying to do. He's probably trying to make a deal with her so that he doesn't have to settle with her in court. He's got the money………..take it. Personally,

I don't like him. And after this bomb incident, you'll have no choice now but to have agents with you at all times."

Adam nodded to Laura, "Okay then Jack, thanks for clearing that up."

"You got it"

And Laura had her answer. "Wait!" Laura yelled. "My mother-n-law"

As they were talking something came to her that never even dawned on her before. Sure she thought about her mother-n-law but never really asked any questions because Edward never wanted to talk about it.

Adam asked, "What?"

She repeated, "Mrs. Jennings."

Jack Larson sounded interested now asked, "who?"

"My mother-n-law. Elizabeth Jennings. She is supposed to be in some home. I was never allowed to visit her. Edward said she went insane after his father was murdered. Every time I brought her up, he always told me to mind my own business, which I thought was totally odd. Someone needs to find her and speak to her without Edward knowing if that's possible."

Jack responded, "We'll definitely make that happen. That might be some valuable information right there. I do vaguely remember the time when that happened. I never was close to Edward just his father. Thanks Laura."

In the meantime, she sat in Adam's office watching Adam pace back and forth trying to figure out what to do next. "Well, we will be taking cabs from now on that's for sure."

"I wonder why my mother-n-law just popped into my head right then and there. That was weird. I've actually thought about finding out what facility she was in and visiting her without Edward knowing. Because I don't believe that she is insane. I think he just didn't want to deal with her anymore after his father was gone so he said she was insane, threw her in a place that would lock her in and drug her up out of convenience. What a piece of crap. With that said, I'm going back to my office to see if I can get some work done."

Adam waved his hand, "oh sure.....sure"

Laura headed for her office. She decided to give Edward a call. "Edward? I'm not going to be able make dinner."

"But why? I really need to speak to you."

"Because I am working late on a new account and someone just blew up my car. Now agents will be escorting me 24/7 until they find whoever is threatening my life and it better not be you. So dinner is going to have to wait. I'm sorry. I have to get to work. Good bye Edward."

He was upset. She wouldn't think Edward would try and cause her harm but doing that to his mother made her think differently. Well, she was feeling a bit uneasy with all that was going on. *Maybe I should have stayed in California.*

She was actually going to give Joe a call just to let him know she was in New York.

"Hi, I just wanted to let you know I'm here and I'm fine."

"Great. Is it nice being back in your office?"

"It would be if people wouldn't be trying to blow me up."

"What? What the hell? What happened?"

"Well, my beautiful car is gone and the FBI is downstairs right now investigating. Adam and I went to go out for lunch and I decided to drive. It was a bit chilly so I decided to turn on the car as we were walking down and Boom. No more car. Someone wanted me dead. Thank God I turned it on when I did."

Joe sounded more than a little concerned, "What is it with you? Do they have ANY ideas who might be after you? And what are they going to do to protect you? You should have just stayed here with me."

She heard the panic in his voice, "It wouldn't have mattered. They are professionals. They would have found me there eventually and I don't have any backup there. Here I have everything I need to stay safe. So, don't worry about me here. They will be caught eventually."

"Okay, as long as you are going to have security twenty four seven."

She sighed, "Yes, I definitely have that. I'm going to get back to work. I just wanted to let you know that I was here and safe."

"Thanks Laura. Make sure you stay safe."

"I will. I promise." And she hung up.

Adam came practically running into her office.

"What's wrong Adam?"

"Jack Larson just called. He and an FBI agent have located Mrs. Jennings. They would like you to go with. They think it would be smart as she would know you as Edward's wife."

"Well, barely. Edward hardly let me see her before we got married and the year we were married before she went into the mental facility but sure, I'll go. I would like to see her again."

Adam picked up the line from Laura's office phone, "yes, she would like to go and speak to Mrs. Jennings. Okay, I will let her know."

He looked at Laura, "They will be picking you up here in thirty minutes. They want to make sure security is high and since they are still downstairs, it's secure."

"Okay. Will Edward be notified about visitors?"

Adam shrugged his shoulders, "That you will have to ask Jack. I'm sure they took every precaution necessary not to spook the jackass because who knows what else he has up his sleeve."

She nodded in agreement, "Yeah, right. Well, I will meet them downstairs in about twenty minutes then."

Adam turned around as he was walking out her door, "And I will be walking down with you. Don't think you will be out of my sights kiddo."

She grabbed her phone and purse and started toward Adam's office. He saw her and started out towards Laura. "Okay kiddo, lets go. And hopefully this time we go down there it will be uneventful" as he raised his eyebrows at her.

They looked at the mess still trying to be sifted through. They had to go way around the tape to get where they had to go. Laura just shook her head as she looked towards her car, "What a mess. How am I even going to explain that to my insurance company? How does that work?"

"You know what? You're not going to worry about that right now. You can take care of that when you get back OR you can call them on your way to the facility. There they are now. Good Luck. I'll see you later."

CHAPTER FOURTEEN

She waved to them and got into the back of the car. "Hi Jack."

"Hi Laura. Laura, this is agent Stevens."

He looked back as much as he could as he was a pretty muscular guy, "How are you Laura?"

"Well, I'd be much better if someone wasn't trying to kill me."

He responded, "We'll get to the bottom of this. This lead may actually turn out to be the icing on the cake."

She had doubts about that, "I don't know about that. She's just an old lady but I never understood why he wouldn't let me see her much when we were together or visit her when she was in the facility. And he would get angry when I would bring it up. So, I just thought maybe there was something to it. I don't know why it came to me."

"Well never the less, the things that people think are meaningless usually end up being the quality witnesses or evidence that we need to break the case wide open so it's good to check it out."

It was quite a ways out. Hidden through hills and woods. It was in a very creepy location. But the worst was yet to come. I think when they all finally got to their final destination their jaws dropped and everyone's hands were clenched to the sides of the doors or the steering wheel for Jack. It was like something you see out of a freaky horror movie.

Jack was the first one to pipe in, "What in the hell is this? Are we even in the right place?" Eternity of Hope Hospital. Yep….we are indeed in the right place."

All Laura could say was, "Of course Edward would put his mother in here. A cold, lifeless, horrible, hidden place."

Agent Stevens opened the door and said, "Let's go."

"Oh, one thing………..Edward isn't going to know anyone visited?" Laura asked quickly.

Jack pulled out an envelope filled with cash. "No, we took care of that."

It was a huge gray stone building that looked to be owned by Dracula himself. They walked inside and it was just as bad inside as it was out.

"Can I help you?" The nurse asked.

Jack replied, "I'm looking for the director, Miss Middleton. I'm Jack Larson and she is expecting us."

"Certainly have a seat and I will get her."

As they waited they looked around.

Agent Stevens cracked a joke, "I'm waiting for a bat to come flying by."

Laura snickered but she also had chills being here and then they heard a horrific scream that made her jump in towards Agent Stevens.

Agent Stevens whispered, "What the fuck was that? I should probably be checking that out." As he got out of his seat, Miss Middleton came walking over.

"Well hello. I'm Miss Middleton and she looked at Jack and said you must be Jack Larson. It's very nice to meet you."

He handed her the envelope of money and just reminded her, "Now remember our deal. This is an investigation and cannot be leaked."

He looked at Laura. "This is Laura and Agent Stevens. Can you show us to Mrs. Jennings please?"

Laura decided to start the questioning, "Why did Mrs. Jennings come here in the first place?"

Miss Middleton seemed very eager to give her the Edward lines of crap, "Well, she couldn't handle her husband's death so her son had no choice but to bring her in here as he had no way to take care of her."

Jack looked at Laura as if to say enough. So, Laura just walked in silence until they came to Elizabeth Jennings door. She was having a panic attack and was starting to sweat a little. *Breathe………breathe…* she thought to herself.

When Miss Middleton unlocked the dungeon door, there her mother-n-law was. Just sitting in her rocking chair reading a book or maybe she was just looking at it. Laura couldn't tell. It was much too dim in here to even read.

"Mrs. Jennings, you have company." Miss Middleton turned to look at the three of them and told them to push the button by the door when they were done and someone would open the door and she left.

Laura was the first one to speak. "Mrs. Jennings? It's Laura Jennings, your daughtern-law. Do you remember me? I tried to come before but Edward wouldn't let me and I want to know why."

Elizabeth Jennings actually looked up at Laura and smiled and softly said, "I remember you. You married Edward."

Laura responded, "Yes, I did. Why did Edward not allow me to see you? Why did he keep me away from you? And why did he put you in this place?"

She started to actually talk, "We had a fight. He said that since father was dead, he was not going to be responsible for coming over and taking care of what father took care of. It was too much work. I was too much work. I said that I would hire people to do some of it but he wouldn't hear of it. He said that people would just steal from me. I told him he was the one who was paranoid and crazy and he got mad and put me in here to shut me up."

He has hidden me from my poor David. I haven't seen or heard from him in over twelve years."

Laura turned around to look at Jack. "Mrs. Jennings? Who is David?" Laura asked with a huge lump in her throat.

Mrs. Jennings looked at her, "He's my other son. Edward's identical twin brother."

At that moment, Laura felt light headed and things started to get darker and darker and the next thing she knew, she was laying on the bed with Jack and Agent Stevens looking over her. "What happened?"

Agent Stevens smirked, "You fainted."

She sat up, "Did I hear Mrs. Jennings say that Edward has a twin brother named David?"

Jack nodded, "Yes."

Laura went back over to Mrs. Jennings. "Dear, are you okay?" she asked Laura.

"Yes, I'm fine. Thank you. Mrs. Jennings? Where does David live and why did Edward never mention ever having a brother?"

Mrs. Jennings folded her hands and looking sad, "Well there was a fall out in the family about twelve years ago and of course it was over money. He made a huge mistake and almost cost Charles his reputation. Charles had to do some major PR work to smooth things over. After that, Charles set David up and told him to do business in Europe and not to return. So, David moved to Europe and has done very well over there with the understanding that he would never show his face here again."

Laura was disgusted, "So they just ousted him out of the family? Who does that? Over money? Who are these people? That is the saddest thing I have ever heard. I think even worse of Edward which I didn't think I could possibly do. Why didn't you tell me what a horrible family I was marrying into? And how can I get you out of here?"

She grabbed Laura's hand. "Why do you think Edward kept us apart? He didn't want us getting too close for fear I might talk. Believe me, I would've told you to run and never look back.   And the only way I can get out of here is with Edward's signature."

Laura looked at Jack. "Clearly, this woman is not insane and doesn't belong here. Is there anything legally that we can do to bypass his damn signature?"

Jack ran his fingers through his hair while he blew out a breath of air, "I have NEVER seen such a soap opera like this in my life. I'm going to need a padded room after this whole thing is over IF I make it. I am going to have to pull some strings and see if we can demand she be seen by a psychiatrist to determine her state of mind and go about it that way instead of fighting to get Edward's signature although with what Mrs. Jennings just told me, I could legally go after him but that would take too damn long."

Laura looked at Mrs. Jennings. "We are going to get you out of here very soon. I promise.

You do not belong here. And one more thing. If anyone asks. No one came in to see you. Okay?" And she gave her a big hug.

They pushed the button and they were let out of the dungeon door. Laura felt horrible for her. She mumbled all the way out the damp, eerie castle.

Agent Stevens got what he needed. He started searching as soon as he got in the car for David. "I'm just wondering if he is, still indeed, in Europe."

Jack added, "Well, Laura said that she found deposit slips with David's name on them in Edward's office. She had no idea what they were."

Laura added, "The deposits were from ten, eleven and twelve years ago."

Jack said, "I had no idea Charles Jennings had another son. And I knew him VERY well."

"Well, I have INTERPOL in on this now as well so they know what is going on and are on the lookout for this guy for questioning", Agent Stevens stated as he continued working.

Laura just sat back and digested what she had just taken in from her poor mother-n-law. She was going to fight for her. That just wasn't fair for her to be locked up like that. And how can a family just disown a son, a brother? Over money?" Disgusting………All about Greed.

Once they returned to Fusion, Inc. Agent Stevens walked her up to the office. "Thank you Agent Stevens for taking me to see my mother-n-law. I hope you got everything you needed to nail Edward and whoever else to the wall."

"I did. I told you it would be important." And he turned and walked out.

She was exhausted. She really didn't want to go to Adam's tonight. Not that she didn't love their family. But she just wanted some peace and quiet. She laid her head down on the desk and heard Adam slowly sneak in. He stood there for a minute.

"How did it go?"

She looked up at him. "Let's see….my poor mother-n-law is locked up in Dracula's castle. We were waiting for bats to fly over our heads. She is not even CLOSE to being insane, she is the sweetest lady EVER and the reason Edward didn't want us to get close is that he has a twin brother who was ousted out of the family twelve years ago over a family fall out about money. He had to move to Europe and was told he could not return here again. His name is…………….get this, David. Edward was afraid his mother would get to close to me and spill the beans. You can close your mouth now."

Adam shook his head quickly, "He has a brother and it never came up? What kind of twisted family did you marry into?"

And then Laura stood up and started getting excited, "I know, I know… that's what I asked her. I asked her why she didn't warn me and she told me that if we had seen more of each other she would have had an opportunity to warn me. And I asked her why Edward put her in that horrible place and she said that they had gotten into a fight after Charles, I mean Mr. Jennings died. Edward told her that he was not going to come over and do what his father used to do as he didn't have time. She assured him she would just hire people to get the things done and Edward got really angry and she said he was the one who was crazy and paranoid, he got mad and ended up taking her there without her permission. She had no say in it at all."

Adam was pacing the floor. "Good God. How do you get her out?"

"The only way is to get Edward's signature. Jack is going to see what else we can do for her like demand she meet with a psychiatrist for a diagnosis but again, I don't know if Edward needs to sign off on that first. Agent Stevens saw her. That is evidence. And she told the whole story in front of both of them so they could go after him criminally somehow but that would take too long."

Adam threw his hands up in the air……..”This is like one big nightmare that just never ends and gets more complicated as we go. Unbelievable."

"I guess INTERPOL is now involved. They are going to try to find David for questioning." It all suddenly clicked, "Yeah…….it all makes sense now. I found a piece of paper shoved way back in one of Edward's drawers and there was transactions from ten, eleven and twelve years ago for David."

Adam asked her, "But if he was no longer considered part of the family, why would Edward be depositing money for him?"

She shrugged her shoulders "Maybe he actually felt bad for him? Or maybe it was from his dad paying him off? Well, once they catch up to him in Europe, they can ask him that million dollar question.   Or they'll have to ask Edward. I just don't know how much more of this I can take before I lose it."

Adam looked at her, "Yeah…I was wondering about that myself. I am pretty worried about you."

"I just need a good night's sleep and I'll be fine in the morning. It's been a day from hell and I'm exhausted."

Adam said "Well, it's getting late. I guess I just need to call down to security to let them know that we are ready and they will send up two agents to drive us to and fro and I'm not sure how many agents will be following us."

She looked at Adam, "I'll stay with you and Gloria tonight but I'm going to have to find a hotel to stay. I love your family. You know that. But I just need some space to grieve and think."

"I understand. You have been through a lot. And I guess if you have a lot of security, you should be fine. Let me call down. Grab your stuff."

They walked down with the agents and hopped in the back of an undercover car. One of the agents spoke, "Okay, I'm Slater and this is Chapman. We'll be the two of the agents taking you back and forth Mrs. Jennings no matter where you go. Depending on the situation, you could have up to six or more agents standing by at any time."

She looked over at Adam, "Well, this should be fun." And sat back took a deep breath, and was quiet for the entire ride. Once they arrived, before they left the car, agent Slater explained that she would have to call down to him first before she left the house and handed him his number. "We will be sitting right outside and there are other agents strategically placed." The agents walked Adam and Laura to the door and made sure the area was secure before they entered the home.

Gloria heard them come in and gave Laura the biggest hug and then hugged her husband. "Are you two okay?" Adam assured her, "Yes, it's fine. There are agents surrounding our house though."

Gloria looked horrified, "What? Why?"

"Honey, Don't worry about it. Everything is fine. I'll fill you in while we sit down for dinner. Laura has had a really hard day."

And Gloria nodded her head, "okay……right." And grabbed Laura's hand. "Come on honey. Come sit down and I'll get you something to eat and a nice strong drink." She looked at her husband "Adam? Can you take her bags and put them in the guest room please?"

Gloria pulled out a chair for Laura, "Sit and I'll get you that drink."

Laura perked up, "Nothing too strong Gloria, maybe just a bottle of wine."

Gloria laughed, "Okay hun, I'll get you that bottle."

Gloria poured Laura and herself a glass of red wine and fixed a drink for Adam and waited for someone to speak. "Okay, what the hell happened?"

Laura looked at Adam and raised her eyebrows, "You tell her. I'm too tired to tell the story."

So, Adam proceeded to tell her the story of the car bomb and what Laura had learned from Mrs. Jennings about Edward having a twin brother and Gloria pretty much looked like Adam did after Laura had laid it all out to him after she returned from the hospital later that day.

Gloria shook her head in disbelief, "That poor woman. And Edward.......what a slime. I never liked him. I knew there was something about him. Didn't I Adam?" And she looked over at him.

And then the "Kevin" subject came up after a few drinks and of course, Laura tried to hold back the tears. She was close enough to Gloria that she told her about her and Kevin and that made it even worse.

Gloria felt awful for Laura, "It wasn't your fault Laura. Imagine seeing your parents murdered right before your eyes and then finding out that your best friends who you trusted for years were the ones who did it and were going to kill you too. They betrayed him in the worst way possible. He shouldn't have taken his life though. He had so much to live for."

And as the girls shed tears, Adam left the room. It was too much for him.

And the evening came to an end and again, Laura softly cried herself to sleep wondering if she was going to make it out of this nightmare herself.

CHAPTER FIFTEEN

Her phone woke her up. She looked and it was a blocked call, "Hello?"

The man on the other line had a raspy voice. No one that she recognized. "Listen to me very carefully. To ensure no harm comes of your parents, you must meet me alone, without any agents following you at your home this afternoon at two. Do you understand?"

Laura getting a little angry about the threat, "It's not my house for another two weeks."

The man on the other line was getting impatient, "Are you taking this seriously? I'll shut this deal down right now and the next time you see your parents they'll be in caskets. I've already taken care of your boyfriend Kevin. Don't push it."

"No...no. I will meet you there at two. No agents. Just me."

And he hung up. She looked at the time. It was four A.M. Her stomach was in knots and her head was racing. *How am I going to possibly get there with no one following me? This is going to be impossible. Do I tell Adam and Gloria? Oh God…………….What am I going to do?*

Of course she couldn't sleep. *What does he mean Kevin? That was a suicide.* She kept thinking about her parents. And wondering who it was on the other end of the phone and how he knew who her parents were and where they lived. Okay. The only way is to let the agents know so they could move her parents to protect them. She called down to agent Slater, "I need to come down and speak to you. I just got a threatening call and we need to do something quickly."

Laura quietly tiptoed down the stairs and out the door and the agents were waiting with the guns drawn to take her to the car. They put her in the back seat and listened.

"I got a call from a blocked number. His voice was raspy. Not someone that I recognize at all. He told me he wants me to meet him alone without any agents………..so he knows you guys are protecting me right now which means he's watching me….at my old house at two P.M today. If I don't do exactly as he says, my parents will die just like he took care of Kevin.

What does he mean by that? I thought that was ruled a suicide."

Agent Chapman immediately called in to let authorities know out there to watch their house and that back up would arrive shortly and that they needed to listen to the recorded call to her phone.

Agent Slater said firmly, "Okay, here is what we are going to do. We are going to set up a safe house for them and move them out of there. You are NOT going to meet this guy at all. We will try and catch him at the location instead. If he senses something is wrong and bails, we'll wait for him to call you back. We will try and track his phone location. If he is too smart and savvy, we may not be able to. But we'll try. At least your parents will be safe. As far as Kevin, we will have to put some calls in about that statement and they will be reviewing the call made to your phone."

Laura felt so relieved, "Okay. I feel so much better about that. My parents were my main priority. Thank you. Make sure they're safe."

The Agents replied, "We will."

They helped her out of the car, guns drawn and very aware of their surroundings and walked her to the door and waited until she locked the door.

She walked back to her room feeling exhausted from the adrenaline rush.

She laid on the bed and just shut her eyes. She just wanted to get a little more sleep before she had to get up. She was so sleep deprived and stressed out and sad. Maybe even depressed. She felt like she was spiraling downward toward a dark abyss of nothingness. *Why does this guy want to kill me? I should just ask him what he wants and just give it to him. I'm tired of all this.*

She heard the kids up. It must be six thirty. Time for school. She waited a little while so that Gloria could get the kids morning started. She didn't want to get up anyhow. She was dreading that inevitable phone call that was sure to have a very angry and spiteful man on the other end threatening her even further.

About seven she headed downstairs. The kids were almost ready to catch the bus. Laura looked at Gloria, "I'm just going to call the agents to let them know that the kids will be out waiting for the bus."

Gloria looked at her funny, "Why would you do that?"

Laura took her aside, "I received a threatening call at four this morning. He threatened my parent's lives if I don't meet him alone today AND he said that he is the one who killed Kevin. I had to go out to speak with the agents this morning and plan for it. I don't know what this guy is capable of. I do know he is watching me because he knows that I have agents following me. I would feel more comfortable if I knew the kids were safe."

Gloria looked at her worried, "Okay...maybe that would be best." And she explained to the kids about the agents so they weren't afraid.

The kids walked out with the agents protecting them.

Gloria looked at Adam, "I'm sorry. This is crazy."

Laura apologetically said, "I know. I told Adam I was going to find a hotel after last night. This isn't fair to your family. I'm really sorry."

Gloria felt bad, "No. I didn't mean it that way. You can stay here as long as you need. I know those agents wouldn't let anything happen to our family. I just have never dealt with anything like this before. That's all."

Adam looked at Laura, "Look kiddo, I feel better knowing you're under my roof than in a hotel room where anything could go wrong. Agents can only do so much. There are too many places to hide in a huge hotel." And he looked at Gloria.

Gloria nodded, "I agree with Adam."

Laura looked at them both, "Are you sure? I just feel like I'm putting you out."

Gloria hugged her, "You're like family to us. You are most definitely not putting us out."

Adam started for the kitchen, "Let's have some coffee, shall we?"

And then Laura's phone rang. It was her parents. "Hi mom."

"I know...I know."

"I don't even know what's going on."

"I guess someone really hates me."

"Mom, it will be fine. Just do what you need to do for now. I know it's inconvenient but I'm trying to save your life here. I love you and I will talk to you when I know more. Love you. Bye."

Laura looked at Gloria and Adam, "Yikes"

Adam teased "Sounds like they're not too thrilled to be pulled out of their comfort zone."

Laura shook her head, "Not at all."

The doorbell rang. Adam excused himself to answer it. It was agent Slater. "May I come in and speak to Mrs. Jennings?"

"Sure, Come on in. Would you like some coffee?"

"No thank you."

Agent Slater addressed Laura, "We are changing shifts. We have briefed Agent Ortega and Davis on everything. However, agent Chapman and I will be re-joining before two so that we can try and take this perpetrator down at two…………best case scenario. We will touch base with the agents around one to make sure everyone is ready to go."

Laura stood up, "Okay, I'm hoping for an easy catch today so we can end this whole nightmare. I guess I'll see you later then."

She plopped herself back down and blew out a breath. "Well, tomorrow is the alimony finalization. Do you think that will at least go smoothly for me?"

Adam looked at her and sipped his coffee, "Knowing Edward, probably not. I'm sure all of his attorneys have something up their sleeves and will make this into a big circus act so that the judge will have no other choice but to push the date back."

Gloria looked into her coffee, "So, are you two working from here today or are you going into the office?"

Adam shrugged his shoulders, "I was actually thinking we might be more secure here than our building. That whole bomb thing yesterday really freaked me out to tell you the truth."

"I have everything I need to work on my account. So, that's not a problem" Laura responded. "Let me get out of my pajamas and I'll meet you back down here with my laptop."

"I'll meet you in my office."

Gloria yelled in to Adam, "So, I guess I'll be serving your breakfast in there?"

"Oh yeah honey. Thanks. That would be great."

So even though they worked in silence, neither one of their minds were on the projects. But at least it kept them busy for a while and they bounced ideas off one another which they hadn't done in a very long time. It was like the old days. It was kind of refreshing.

Twelve O'clock came around and Laura's stomach immediately turned into butterflies and Adam saw it on her face. "Let's take a little intermission. I say it's time for a cocktail to calm your nerves."

When they emerged from the office to the dining room, Gloria was just fixing lunch for everyone. Adam pulled out wine and wine glasses for the three of them and poured.

Gloria brought the food in and saw the wine. "What's this all about?"

Adam handed her a glass, "To settle the nerves."

Gloria pushed some food towards Laura, "Here darling eat."

"I'm so nervous, I can't but thank you. I'll try in a little while."

Gloria looked at Adam, "You will eat."

"Sure. Hand me a plate please."

As time seemed to tick away so slowly, the doorbell rang. It was agent Slater and agent Davis.

Agent Slater didn't waste any time, "Mrs. Jennings, this is what is happening today. Agent Chapman and I are going to the home to see if we can catch this guy. We have to move quickly here as we have to move in discreetly. Agent Davis here and Ortega are going to be in here with you just in case we don't get him as I'm sure a call will be coming through. They will be monitoring your phone. There will be other agents outside. Got it?"

She just nodded.

Agent Slater turned and left leaving agent Davis there. Two minutes later agent Ortega came walking in announcing himself.

Agent Davis asked Laura if he could see her phone. He took the back off and inserted a small device in it and said, "This should do it."

Laura looked at him questioningly, "Do what exactly?"

"It will record the conversation and we'll have his voice so we can look for voice recognition. I know your phone is tapped but this will hopefully capture his location. Once he calls IF they don't catch him we'll have to work fast to find his location if we can. This is what this computer is for" and he pointed.

Gloria got up to go to the kitchen, "Well let's hope they catch the bastard."

As it was nearing two O'clock everyone but the agents were pacing the floor.

Laura asked them, "Now if something happens and this guy does call, do you want me to put him on speaker?"

Both agents responded, "Sure."

Agent Davis got a call, "Yeah, Davis."

"Nothing huh? You think he has eyes watching?"

"Where were you hiding?"

"He must have watched or had her watched up until now and knew she never left."

"Okay, we'll expect the call, and agent Davis hung up the phone.

He looked around, "Well, you all heard that. This guy has people working for him I'm assuming and as soon as he gets wind that your parents are not home, it will enrage him so that he may make a mistake."

Agent Ortega added in, "And because he will more than likely go to a secure place, we don't expect a call from him for a while."

Meanwhile Agent Slater and Chapman joined them and waited for the call.

The kids arrived home from school and was shocked to see all the agents set up in their dining room. Gloria grabbed them some snacks and sent them off to their rooms to start their homework.

Just as they expected, the call came. Laura pushed speaker. He spoke first, "Okay bitch. Remember, you're still playing my game now and you just threw down the wrong card."

Her voice was shaky, "What is it that you want from me?"

He impatiently sighed, "You know too much. You got too close and too lucky and now you have to pay the price. Oh……..and just so you know, your California boyfriend is dead. What's his name? Joey? Yeah…..Sorry about that. I told you. You're playing my game and you play by my rules so the next time I tell you to do something, you do it." And he hung up.

Laura immediately tried calling Joe, it kept going to his voicemail. "This can't be happening." She looked at Adam with tears in her eyes and screamed, "This can't be happening!!! What the fuck does he want from me!!!!"

The look on her face was neither sadness nor grief. It was madness. She had finally made it to that last piece left of her sanity and right then and there she lost her self and it took all four agents to take her down. "Get the fuck off of me!!!! My life is over!!!! My life is nothing….My life is nothing." And she was hysterically crying.

Gloria looked at Adam, "Maybe I should call a doctor? Do you know a good psychiatrist? What do you want me to do?"

Adam looked down and shook his head in despair, "God Gloria, give her a little time."

One of the agents looked at them and said, "It wouldn't hurt to take her to the hospital to have her checked out."

Laura screamed, "NO!, I'm not going to end up like Elizabeth Jennings. I'm NOT going to the hospital."

The agents were able to let her go. Gloria came down by her side, "Laura, Can Adam and I just take you for a ride?"

She pulled one of the agents aside, "Could two of you help us get her to the hospital so you can help us get her in? She needs to be checked out."

Agent Chapman agreed, "Sure, that's probably best."

Adam grabbed her phone just in case and purse and one agent drove with Adam in the front while the other agent sat in back with Gloria in the back with Laura in between them. They were totally breaking protocol but they needed to get her in without her hurting herself and causing injury to people around her.

CHAPTER SIXTEEN

Once at the hospital, it was a scene to say the least. They had to give her something right away to keep her from hurting herself, the nurses and doctors along with strapping her down for extra precaution. Seeing her like that just tore at Adam's heart. He knew how much she had gone through and she was like a little sister to him and he hated when she was hurting.

When they had to sedate her, her shirt had come up and Gloria and Adam saw the healing lacerations all over her body and gasped. The doctors and nurses started asking questions about it as well so Adam had to tell them what had happened so they could verify their story.

As they waited in the waiting room. Gloria grabbed Adam's hand, "I had NO idea that she was beaten that badly. Her poor body. She went through hell and pure torture. Those boys better never see the light of day."

Adam was in deep thought, "I thought about what she might have gone through. She didn't want to show me and now I know why. That is nothing near from what I had imagined. That is much worse. That poor girl. She has every right to have a breakdown right now. Everything that has happened to her. And now she loses Joe? The one good thing left in her life that she was looking forward to after this whole thing with Edward was finalized is gone. She needs time to heal. I am taking over her account. She is off of work indefinitely. She deserves to take as much time as she needs right now because she has always been there for me when I've needed her for anything. My number one in my company." And he broke down and cried.

Gloria had never seen him like this. "I'm sorry Adam. I know. I know. She doesn't deserve any of this." And she held him.

Gloria said, "Well, we could probably get a message to her parents but there is no sense in getting them all worried if they can't do anything anyway. They won't let them leave the safe house."

Adam making sure he still had Laura's phone said, "I hope they figure out who this guy is quick. He said she got too close. Knows too much. Would that mean Kevin? Because she knows who killed Kevin's parents? That doesn't make sense. Did she meet another of Kevin's friends? I don't know."

One of the doctors came out to let them know that she was resting and they could go in to see her.

Gloria entered first, "Hi honey. How are you feeling?"

And Laura started crying, "I'm sorry. I'm sorry I lost it." She looked at Adam. "Joe is gone. Why? Why is this man doing these horrible things? Now little Genevieve has no daddy because of me. And this was the only hope I had left in my life. What have I done so wrong that I deserve all this pain?" She was so drugged her words were slurred and her eyes were half shut.

Adam pulled a chair over to her bed, "You have done everything right in your life. I have no reason why these things are happening to you. Maybe because you are associated with a horrible husband."

Laura put her hands over her heart, "I have no more left to give in this heart of mine because the people that I truly gave it to are now gone. I am an empty soul full of sorrow and burden. I just want to fall asleep and never wake up."

"You don't mean that Laura" Gloria said quickly. "We'll get you some help, okay?"

Adam gave Laura a hug, "Now kiddo, I'm taking your purse and phone home with me so they're safe okay?"

"What if Joe tries calling me?"

Gloria and Adam looked at each other and Gloria gave her a hug and said, "Don't worry about that, we'll let him know. Get some rest honey and we will see you in the morning."

As they walked down the hall, Adam said, "Geez, it must be the medicine she's on. Poor kid. I hope she feels better in the morning."

They met the agents in the waiting room and hitched a ride back to the house as they gave them an update on Laura. They felt just as bad for her. "Tough break", one of the agents commented.

Adam pulled out Laura's phone, "I do have her phone just in case."

Agent Ortega looked, "okay great. Did you call a couple of the agents to let them know to take the hospital?"

"Did that on the way over" Agent Chapman responded. He looked at Adam and Gloria, "There will also be new agents outside your place again. He seems to be targeting people close to Laura so we are being overly precautious."

"Okay" Adam said.

The agents packed up and out they went.

Gloria checked on the kids and came back down to throw something quick on for a late dinner. Adam looked at Gloria, "I don't know about you but I feel like I worked a twenty hour day. I'm eating and heading up. I'll go up and see if the kids need help with their homework."

Adam came running back down the stairs......"Shoot!"

"What? What's the matter?"

Adam rubbed his face, "Tomorrow was supposed to be the alimony finalization. I need to call Jack right now. Damn it."

Adam went in to his office to try and get a hold of Jack Larson on his cell phone. He didn't answer so Adam had to leave a message letting him know that Laura was in the hospital and she was in pretty bad shape. "Call me back Jack."

He walked back into the dining room. "Anything else?"

"Did you get a hold of him?"

"Nope. Had to leave a message. Hope he gets it and calls me back."

It was good that Adam went to bed early as he was awoken in the night a couple of times by nightmares but was able to fall right back to sleep. Morning came and he felt rested. He got up with kids and helped get them ready for school when Laura's phone started ringing.

He looked at Gloria and then looked down at the number. He shrugged his shoulders. Gloria impatiently said, "Answer it."

"Hello?"

The young man on the other line asked, "May I ask who this is?"

"This is Laura's boss Adam."

"Hi Adam, I've heard a lot about you. Is Laura there?"

Adam was very confused, "May I ask who this is please?"

"Sure, it's Joe."

"Joe? We thought you were……Laura had a little breakdown after she was told that you were dead. She is in the hospital right now resting. She tried calling you several times."

"Well, what happened was my friend Warren who is a police officer got wind somehow that there were other counties contacted by your people up there warning them to get me out to a safe house as I was in danger. He grabbed me and took me somewhere safe telling me to leave my phone behind so I couldn't be located. That's why she couldn't get a hold of me. I had to go through channels just to get Laura's number. Is Laura okay?"

"I haven't seen her since last night but I think she'll be okay because you my friend, you are getting the next flight out here."

"I just don't have the money for that right now."

"Joe, I will book you a first class ticket. You just tell Warren? Is it? so that he knows and an agent will pick you up from the airport and take you to the hospital. She needs to see you. You have no idea. Is this the number you can be reached at?"

"Yes sir."

"I will call you back as soon as the ticket is reserved."

Gloria was jumping up and down. "He is okay? This is so great."

Gloria grabbed Adam's arm, "Aren't we taking chances by bringing him here in the line of fire?"

"You know what Gloria? Laura needs this more than anything right now. This will be positive towards her wellbeing. I will make it happen."

As he made the arrangements, Gloria finished getting the kids ready and out the door for the bus.

While that was happening, Jack finally called him back. "Hey Jack. Yeah, she is pretty bad right now and is not going to be able to make it to court today."

Jack laughed, "Doesn't matter, Edward is being questioned right now for some of this other stuff that just came to light. The FBI is digging a little deeper into his past so he will not make it either. It's been postponed until Monday. Will that work for Laura?"

Adam was pretty sure she would be fine by then, "I think Monday will work."

"Well if something comes up Adam, let me know first thing Monday morning and we can do something then."

"Okay sounds good Jack. Thanks."

Jack added, "Oh by the way, they are still trying to find David Jennings and apparently he is no longer in Europe so they are still trying to locate him as well for questioning."

"Okay, good to know."

He had found a flight for Joe, he was going to call him to see if he could make it and then book it for him.

He called the number and Warren answered. "Is this Warren?" Hi Warren, this is Adam Grant. I'm working with the agents here. Could you get Joe a pre-paid phone for his trip? That way we know when he arrives at the airport so the agents can pick him up quickly and promptly. Thanks. Now can I speak with Joe?"

"Joe, I found a flight for you. It leaves at ten AM non-stop which will put you here at eight thirty PM and we'll take you right over to the hospital. Will that work for you?"

"Yes, that sounds great. And thank you so much for doing this. There is nothing I want more than to be by her side when she needs me most."

Quickly Adam added, "Make sure you let me know what your new pre-paid phone number is so I have some kind of contact with you. Warren said he was going to take care of it."

"No problem."

"Now I need to speak to Warren again. Warren I need your information so I can send the ticket your way for Joe. Make sure he is secure."

"He'll have everything he needs" Warren assured him.

"Thanks Warren."

After that was done. There was a sense of hope and a moral comeback for Laura. She was going to defeat the devil that she had married and save all the others that were falling into his evil money powered grip.

Adam was going to wait until one of the other agents who were familiar with the account of last night's happenings came back on shift so he could let them know what had transpired and what was planned for the day.

Adam and Gloria were planning on going to the hospital that morning. Since Joe would be coming in that evening, he wanted the nurses to tone down the medication if they could so she wasn't so out of it when he came in to see her. I'm sure he would understand anyhow. Gloria was going to take make-up and hair stuff in this afternoon and work on her appearance (not that she needed it) but just a little sprucing up.

She looked at Adam. "Well, we'll see how she is this morning. Maybe I can see if one of the hair stylists would be willing to come in or something if she is doing better. Maybe we should tell her that Joe is coming in."

"I don't think she'd believe us. I don't think she knows what to believe anymore. The poor kid is so confused it would just be easier to keep it quiet until he just comes walking in. He is just what she needs right now. I have never seen that girl in such a fragile state. She has taken a whole lot and has kept her composure through it all.

Let's go see if they have changed shifts yet."

They walked out the door and saw agent Slater and Chapman. They slid into the back seat.

"Good morning" agent Slater said.

"I'm guessing you are heading to the hospital" agent Chapman added.

"Indeed we are. And I just wanted to let you know that Joe got very lucky" Adam said.

Agent Chapman asked "So he is alive?"

"Yes. Apparently, because your agency is so thorough, knowing about Joe because Laura had spoken about him to you and her tapped phone and learning of this new information about Kevin possibly being this guy's first murder, authorities were alerted in California that he may be in danger. They were told to find him a safe house and to make a long story short, he ended up with his friend Warren who is a police officer."

Slater said, "So, once they knew he was going after people that were close to her, our agency started working fast."

Adam added, "One more thing, Edward is being questioned today on things that just came to light like his brother."

Chapman snickered, "Yeah, we heard about that."

"And I bought a first class ticket so that Joe could fly out here to see Laura. She needs that more than anything right now. Can an agent pick him up from the airport around eight thirty? If not, I will pick him up."

Slater shook his head, "No, an agent will most definitely pick him up. We don't need any blood on our hands on our time. That girl has had enough to deal with."

"We are getting closer to who this guy is. I can feel it. Just a few more things we need and we will have him" Chapman said with confidence.

Gloria spoke up for the first time, "Good. I want one good kick in the nuts to show him how much of an evil bastard he is."

Everyone started laughing hysterically. She was so quiet the entire time and that was the first thing out of her mouth.

Slater, still laughing said, "Gloria, if we can do that for you, I will make sure you get your shot at him. I promise."

When they got to the hospital, Adam spoke to the nurses to find out how she had done during the night before proceeding to her room.

When Adam and Gloria entered her room, she was still sleeping. They walked in anyway as they had stopped and grabbed some good food on the way in. They just sat down and turned on the TV while they drank their coffee. They were in no rush and wanted to be present when she awoke.

A few minutes later, Laura's phone rang and Adam hurried out of the room to take the call. "Hello?"

"Okay, Joe I have your number. I look forward to seeing you. Have a safe flight" and Adam quietly came back into the room, smiled and whispered to Gloria, "It was just Joe. Everything is fine."

Just then the nurse came in to check on Laura's IV. Adam felt this was the perfect time to speak to someone about her medication. "Is she still being sedated?"

The nurse was looking at her chart. "At this point in time, yes she is. The nurses were told to decrease the dose during the evening hours but she is still sedated until further notice. The doctor will be in to see her this afternoon to check on her again."

Adam stood up, "So I guess I will have to speak to the doctor then. Do you know who the doctor on call is or approximately when he might be in to see her?"

"It's Doctor Michaels but I'm not sure when he would be doing his rounds. I can look at the schedule and try to pin point an approximate time for you. You'll more than likely be waiting a while.

"That's fine. Just let me know when he comes in and I will be here. I am willing to wait."

"Okay. I'll be right back" the nurse said as she strode out the door.

Gloria looked at him, "Well, make sure you bring something to do and eat for you and Laura."

The nurse came back in "Doctor Michaels is coming in at two today."

"Thank you."

Just then, Laura opened her eyes and saw Gloria and Adam. "Hi" she said groggily. "I feel weird. What do they have me on?"

Gloria walked over to her and brushed her hair back, "How are you feeling other than weird?"

Laura looked at Adam as he walked over, "Very sad. I'm not even sure why I'm in here. What happened?"

Gloria and Adam looked at each other not knowing how to answer that question. But Adam decided to answer cautiously.

"Remember when you said that you didn't know how much more you could take? And I told you that I was concerned you were going to have a break down because you were holding it all in and trying to be tough?"

She put her hands to her face, "Oh no. I had a nervous breakdown last night?"

Gloria grabbed her hands, "its fine. Your brain can only take so much stimulation. The main thing is you're okay now."

Gloria looked at Adam, "You may as well tell her. She seems like she is well now."

Adam smiled, "Do you know what triggered your reaction last night?"

Laura shook her head, "No, I can't recall."

"Okay. You got a call saying Joe was gone."

"Wait! I do remember that. Oh my god."

"No Laura, Wait....Joe is not dead. He is on his way here to see you."

Laura looked at him with a look of desperation in her eyes, "What?"

Adam nodded, "Yes. I booked him a first class ticket."

"But how?" was all she could say.

"Well, apparently, since you had sat down with one of the agents and Jack and spoke about Joe Venetti at length and they knew this guy was targeting people close to you, they notified the proper authorities in California so that they could get Joe to a safe place and he happened to call your phone from that safe place and I answered it."

Laura started to get out of the bed. "I need to get out of here."

Gloria stopped her. "Whoa. Not yet. The doctor will be in to see you this afternoon and Joe will be here to see you around nine O'clock hopefully to get you out of here."

Laura then covered her mouth, "Oh my gosh. My court appearance is today. I'm going to miss it. I've got to get out of here."

Adam tried to calm her, "Laura, you are getting worked up about everything when you are supposed to be resting. It was postponed to Monday because Edward was pulled in for questioning today by the FBI."

"Oh. Really?" and she laid back and started to feel the effects of the medicine again.

"We brought in some food for you that we thought you'd like since the food here is mediocre. Would you like a bagel with cream cheese?" Gloria asked.

"Sure" Laura said tiredly.

Gloria fixed her one and Adam and her ate with Laura and told her they would be back that afternoon.

CHAPTER SEVENTEEN

As the evening came and it was time to pick up Joe from the airport, Adam was nervous and also very excited for Laura. He had gotten a good report from Doctor Michaels that afternoon so she would either be able to come home that evening or the next morning.

The agents parked and Adam and one of the agents walked in while the other stood watch by the car to get Joe. It was a smooth transaction. They got in the car and headed to the hospital. The one thing that was on Adam's mind was the fact that this "guy" whoever he was, has gone into hiding and they hadn't heard a word from him. That was making him nervous. Obviously this guy knew what he was doing.

"Thank God nothing happened to you Joe. Whoever this guy is, is making Laura's life and everyone around it a living hell. Her parents are in a safe house too."

"I didn't know what to think.   I had to call into my employer to tell them that I'm in hiding as per FBI orders because someone wants to kill me. It sounds made up but I had to do what I had to do."

Once they got to the hospital, they arrived to her room and she was in very good spirits. Joe walked over to her and hugged her and wouldn't let go. "I missed you so much Laura."

"Adam feeling a little uncomfortable just said, "I'll be out in the waiting room for a while."

Joe sat down on her bed next to her and leaned in and kissed her. "What in the world happened here?"

She raised her eyebrows, "You have no idea. I don't even know where to begin. It started with the car bomb and then the killer told me he killed Kevin and it wasn't a suicide."

Joe was about to say something and Laura put her hand up to stop him. "No wait there is more. When I told the FBI about how Edward would never let me see Mrs. Jennings and every time I would bring up the so-called mental institution he put her in, he would get mad at me and change the subject. That was one of the things.

So, they decided it would be worth going and speaking to Mrs. Jennings."

And when I found out about Edward's twin brother David, it all made sense to me. When I found the deposits with Brandi's name on them in Edward's office, I also found a piece of paper back in one of his drawers with transactions listed for a David that were done ten, eleven and twelve years ago. I didn't think anything of it. But after she said that it all made sense. Those deposits were made to his brother. But now I'm wondering why after the fall out, Edward or his father would be sending him large deposits. Was he still being paid off to stay in Europe?"

And Laura continued to tell Joe about everything that she learned and he could not believe it.

The first thing out of his mouth was, "You need to get that poor lady out of there."

Laura agreed, "I know but Edward has the upper hand in that. My attorney was supposed to do some research to see if there was anything we could do. Our court date is on Monday. If you would like to come to support me, that would be fine with me. I just want this finalized."

"But Laura, what about this killer that is still out there?"

She shrugged her shoulders, "Everyone involved may have to change their names and move. I don't really know. I'm sure my parents are NOT going to be happy but if they can't catch him, I can't live in fear. This guy is like a nomad. He is off the map."

She looked at him and took a deep breath, "Okay now that I caught you up on everything, how are you?"

He smiled, "Better than you. Are you okay?"

"I'm good now" and he hugged him. "I'm ready to get out of here."

Joe looked at her, "Yeah?"

"Yeah."

"Let me go talk to Adam and see if we can arrange that. I'll be right back."

The weekend went by quickly and she couldn't wait for Monday to be done and over with.

There were more agents than you could count at the court that day. Joe did come with. There were agents inside, outside, in the hallways, sitting on either sides of Laura and front and back of her.

As they sat in front of the judge, Edward looked over at her several times with eyes glaring. She didn't understand why. They were cordial last time she saw him. Maybe he got wind that she had visited his mother. She didn't care. It wasn't her fault, it was all his. Who treats their brother and mother like that? How can you betray family? It's bad enough he did what he did to her but what he did to his mother and brother was unforgivable. But she was here to break ties with him and get his mom out of that dreadful place. It was just the matter of the alimony which she was sure he was NOT happy about. Both attorneys had the paperwork in front of them as did the judge showing the alimony Laura was entitled to when suddenly, Edward excused himself and stood up, looked at Laura and said, "This is Edward's payback" and it was so quick, he pulled it and fired a shot directly at Laura but one of the agents stepped in front of her and shots were fired directly into Edward and he was down."

All Laura heard, were agents calling "shots fired!! Shots fired!! And agents were rushing inside as she was on the ground. The agent in front of her was bleeding. He had been shot in the shoulder by Edward. She grabbed her scarf and put pressure on his wound as other agents were yelling agent down. The paramedics arrived within minutes. The scene was chaotic. Joe came rushing over to Laura. She had so many questions but she didn't know where anyone was. "Joe, was that David? Was that Edward's twin brother?"

"No one is giving me any answers. They are trying to locate Edward right now. It's a man hunt. I guess we know who was trying to kill you."

Laura moved through the chaos to find her attorney. "Jack………..Jack", she was trying to get through the crowd. "What in the hell happened?"

"Well, I'm thinking that was his brother David. And this is one big mess."

Laura saw the paramedics working on David, "Is he going to make it?"

Jack looked over there, "If he does, he is never going to see the light of day. I just want some answers."

"I would like some answers as well" Laura added.

Jack threw his hands up, "Let's see what I can do."

It didn't take long before the authorities found Edward. He was in the penthouse tied up in the bedroom. David told him he was going to kill Laura and he had someone coming for him. But apparently, Trevor, Kevin's so-called friend didn't have it in him. Edward explained to the police that he feared his brother would someday come back for revenge as David was forced and threatened to leave by their father who was a very powerful man.

After Trevor heard what happened, he immediately went to police to tell them everything. He was afraid Jonah and Jose` would talk in prison and turn him in. He explained that David had befriended Jonah and Jose` in Europe and recruited and prepped them for the murder of Charles Jennings but when they came to the US, they set up in California where they met Kevin and became friends with him. And after being at his parent's home where he lived at the time and getting to know them, they figured they would kill his parent's as their first conquest. They recognize they were wealthy and by that time they were familiar with the house and knew where everything was.

Then they met Trevor and he acted as a watch dog. The next break-in was the one in Chicago which he was there for five years ago and then Edward's dad, Charles, three years ago and then this whole ordeal with Kevin and Laura in California and then the planned killing of Edward.

Trevor also told him that because Jonah and Jose` failed their mission, that David actually went to California to finish Kevin off himself to make it look like a suicide.

And as far as David's mother went, he hated her just as much as the rest of his family for not saying or doing anything. He felt that she should have stepped up to her own husband and not allowed him to make such an impetuous decision all because of his reputation was at stake for a mistake that he made. It was a significant one but he was willing to put in the time to make it right. But his father didn't want him around after that. His father paid off him to leave the US and never come back and threatened him that if he did come back he would never work in investments or anything related again. Not after the huge error he made. And she just let him go.

Needless to say, David Jennings did not make it to the hospital. He was pronounced dead before he arrived which was a real loss for Laura. She had so many questions for him that no one else could answer but him.

Edward was looking at fraud for holding his mother in a mental hospital without a proper diagnosis and was sentenced to three years in jail and a $100,000 fine. But finding out that his own brother planned the murder of his father, murdered his girlfriend and was planning on murdering him tortured Edward.

Laura and Jack Larson drove to Eternity of Hope Hospital with all the necessary paperwork.

Laura was so excited to be able to get her out of there. "Well, here it goes. I can't wait to see the looks on the nurses faces when you hand them the paperwork."

They walked into this forbidden place and they asked to speak to Miss Middleton. "Sure, one moment."

Laura's stomach was so nervous. Jack saw her fiddling. "Calm down." And then they heard the footsteps.

"Ah, hello again. What can I do for you? Are you visiting Mrs. Jennings today?"

Jack Larson handed her the paperwork, "Not today. We are actually removing her from this facility. You will find all the necessary legal paperwork is in order."

She looked at the paperwork and then at Jack confused, "I really don't see how this is happening as Mr. Jennings really needs to sign her out of here."

Jack rocked back and forth on his feet, "Well, Mr. Jennings is in jail and has confessed to admitting Mrs. Elizabeth Jennings to a mental hospital without proper diagnosis and you Miss Middleton were paid off also monthly to keep your mouth shut as well. You may be looking at jail time yourself so I wouldn't be asking too many questions at this point because the cat is out of the bag."

The look on her face was priceless. "Right this way."

She unlocked the door. Laura not trusting her said, "Jack, stand by the door while Mrs. Jennings and I gather her things. I don't want that horrible woman locking us in here."

"Oh yeah…….I never thought of that."

"Mrs. Jennings. I have good news. You're going home. Let's pack your stuff."

She looked at Laura with tears in her eyes and grabbed her hands and Laura helped her stand up. Mrs. Jennings gave her a hug and cried "I'm really going home? To my home?"

"Yes. To your home. We'll get you all set back up in there. I'll hire a cleaning company to help you dust or whatever you need."

She started to get a little pep in her step. "You dear are something else. I have not felt this alive in a long time. I don't need a cleaning crew. I have enough energy to clean that whole house."

Laura giggled and looked at Jack. "Well, okay then. Let's get out of this dungeon. And just so you know, you don't have to worry about your evil son, he's in jail for now."

"Good. That's where he belongs. What about David?"

"Well, the agents had to protect me. Unfortunately, David tried to kill me. There's a lot more to the story. I'm so sorry Mrs. Jennings. We can talk about it after we get you settled in your home."

Mrs. Jennings just bowed and shook her head. What has my family become? Nothing but greed and deceit fill their souls."

Laura put an arm around her, "Well you still have me. I'm a pretty good person."

Mrs. Jennings giggled probably for the first time in years and said, "You rescued me from here. I would say you are a great person. Now let's go."

As they drove her home, she was so excited and relieved. Laura asked her, "Do you think Edward sold your car or do you think your car is still in the garage?"

"Who knows with him. It's probably still in there."

Laura said, "Well, I can take you grocery shopping so you have something in the house."

She looked at Laura, "Do you know how good that sounds. Grocery shopping. I can buy whatever I want. I can make or bake whatever I want. Wonderful."

Jack helped them take everything in. "Is there an extra key hidden somewhere?" Jack asked.

"Hold on....let me think" Mrs. Jennings said.

"Over there, underneath that statue there should be a key. No one knew about it but me."

Sure enough it was still there. Laura grabbed it and cleaned the dirt off the best she could.

They unlocked the door and it was pretty dusty. "Oh my poor house. It needs a good cleaning that's for sure. Oh how I missed my house. I cannot WAIT to sleep in my own bed again."

She hugged Laura again. "If it wouldn't have been for you. I would have been in there for the rest of my life. Thank you so much."

Laura smiled, "You don't have to thank me. I knew what I had to do and made sure I did it. You belong here. So let's get you settled and see if your car is here and if it runs so we can get you some food."

Sure enough, her Bentley was still in the garage. Laura asked her for the keys. "Hold on sweetie. They should be in the study."

So Laura waited. "Here they are."

Laura turned the key and it started right up. "Huh. For not running in a few years, that's pretty impressive. Jack, you can go. No need to stick around. Jack, one more thing………..thank you."

"You are welcome. I'll call you when I get the legal paperwork for the alimony and whatever else we have coming to us. I'm glad this mess is almost over. I'll see you later."

Off the two of them went for groceries. Laura just wanted to make sure Mrs. Jennings was able to take care of herself and was of sound mind and after spending almost the whole day with her, Laura saw what a spunky little lady she actually was and she was going to be just fine. "Well I'll be back tomorrow to check on you, okay?"

"Sure dear. That would be fine."

She took the Bentley back to her place and opened the door and smelled something cooking. "Hello?"

Joe came to greet her and gave her a big kiss. "This house is not bad at all. It all depends on who you are sharing it with."

She started to get nosey and walked towards the kitchen, "What's cooking?"

"You'll see. How did you get here?"

"Oh, Mrs. Jennings let me borrow her Bentley."

"What? Her Bentley? Nice. Is she happy to be back? That poor lady."

Laura laughed, "That poor lady is spunkier than a squirrel trying to find its nut. We went grocery shopping and she went crazy in there. We had two carts full of food. She will be just fine."

CHAPTER EIGHTEEN

He pulled her close to him and kissed her neck. "Now that all this is over, I want to show you how much I missed you and how much I care about you and how much Laura...........I love you."

"She looked at him, "Oh yeah? Well, I would like to show you how much I missed you and how much I care about you and how much...........I love you."

And they kissed so passionately, they fell against the kitchen island. Laura looked at the stove, "What about the food?"

Joe turned off the burners, "It can wait." And he picked her up and took her into the living room and laid her on the couch. "How are your cuts? Can I look at them first?"

She assured him, "They're fine." And she lifted her shirt and he tried not to cringe.

"I don't want to make love to you if you are still in pain."

"I'm fine" and she grabbed his face to bring his lips down to meet hers and they kissed as he fondled her breasts. And things started to heat up. Laura could feel everything getting hot and wet. Joe laid down next to her and she felt him. He was ready for her. He slowly moved his hand down her pants and she let out a moan. He played with her down there teasing her a little getting her ready for him. She was ready. She wanted to ride him so bad. She unbutton his jeans and started to unzip is pants. She couldn't wait any longer he slid his jeans and boxers off and she sat on him and started. It didn't take but thirty seconds and she came. She looked at him with fire in her eyes and he knew, "keep going baby" and she did. She let out all of her frustrations five more times. But he couldn't hold out. "I have to come" and she rode him so fast and hard they both came together. The satisfaction she felt was unbelievable.

She laid on him and both of their hearts were pounding. He joked with her, "You were like an animal. What happened?"

She playfully smacked him, "I don't know. I can't say that I'm sorry though."

He started getting dressed when Laura's phone rang. "Oh it's my parents. I have to take this. Hi mom."

Grace asked "Where have you been? Are you okay?"

"Yes. I'm fine. Are you okay? How is dad? Did he survive the safe house?"

Grace replied, "Yeah, we were more than fine. But we really didn't get any details. Now what happened? I did hear that Edward went to jail. That's where the bastard belongs. This whole thing was absurd. We were hearing things but there was no way to get a hold of you. Do you know how frustrating that is?"

I know mom. I'm sorry. This whole ordeal has been crazy. I found out that twelve years ago there was a fallout between Mr. Jennings, Edward and his twin brother, David."

Her mother started screaming on the phone, "What? He has a brother? And no one ever told you? Why? Why the secret?"

"I don't know. He was sent away to Europe by his father because he screwed up bad and almost ruined the Jennings name. So, Mr. Jennings bought him out and sent him off and told him never to come back."

Grace started freaking out, "What? Oh my God. What is this family?"

"Well, it gets better mom. You know how I told you Edward had to lock up his mom in a mental hospital because she was insane?"

"Yes, I remember you saying that."

"Well, it's not true. He locked her up in a dungeon so that she wouldn't open her mouth about all the family secrets and he admitted it to the FBI so I got her out of there and back into her home today. Now he is spending three years in jail for fraud and has to pay $100,000 in fines.

Grace was silent for a moment, "That poor lady. You married into a freaking evil family. Your father always knew there was something about Edward and he was right. What about the shooting in the courtroom? Were you in there? I was worried sick."

"Yes, David had tied Edward up and he had people working with him so someone else was supposed to take Edward out while he showed up to court pretending to be Edward to take me out but instead, he was the one that was taken out. And the guy who was supposed to kill Edward ended up coming in to talk to the police and telling them everything."

Her mom sighed, "Is this over now? Is the drama over? Because I can't take anymore. I could actually write a book about all this. Maybe I will."

"Yes, I know mom. But it's all over now. And remember Joe Venetti? The one I almost married eight years ago? The sweet one?"

Grace sounding cautious said, "Yes, I remember. He was really nice. We liked him."

"Well, weird enough, I ended up meeting up with him in California and we caught up and now he's here with me in New York." And she whispered, "He's cooking dinner for me."

Grace started screaming into the phone, "What? He's there right now? And he's cooking for you? Hold on to that guy. Bring him over here again. Oh my gosh your father is going to be so happy."

"There's one thing mom. He's got a three year old daughter in California so I might be moving there."

Grace was very disapproving, "No. You can't move that far away from us. We'll see you less than we see you now. No. Not going to happen. Can't Joe bring his daughter out to New York?"

"Mom, she does have a mother."

Grace sighed, "Don't make any decisions yet. Please."

"Fine. I'll talk to you later. Love you. Bye"

Joe walked in, "I caught a little of your conversation. They don't want you to move?"

"Nope."

He hugged her, "Yeah, we really haven't talked about the arrangements or plans yet sooooo is this something we want to do tonight or tomorrow because I should probably be getting back to my job before I get fired."

"She looked at him, "I don't think you are going back to work. We'll talk about it later. Let's eat."

As they sat down to eat, Laura made a suggestion, "Do you think since we have this huge house anyways, Jennifer would let us fly back to get Genevieve and bring her back here for a couple of weeks? That way she doesn't have to worry about paying for childcare and I will have hopefully all the paperwork finalized and we'll have more of an idea of what we are doing. What do you think?"

Joe thought about it, "That actually sounds like a good idea. I'm not sure if Jennifer would want her to go for two weeks but it doesn't hurt to ask."

"Okay. Give her a call after we're done eating. It will be great. I need a new car too. I have to call the insurance company and tell them someone blew up my car."

Joe smiled at her, "So, what do I tell Jen when she asks me why I'm not working? You know she's going to ask because I never have vacation."

"You just tell her, that you have more important things to pursue. I don't know. Tell her you're working for me as a marketing assistant. I'm teaching you the ropes. Make something up. You are giving me some babies." And Laura started laughing.

They started cleaning the kitchen and Laura said, "Go ahead and call Jennifer and speak to Genevieve. I'll finish cleaning up in here. And then I'm going to start cleaning out Edward's office because it's now MY office."

After she was done in the kitchen she reluctantly moved into the dreaded office. She assumed he'd been in there since she'd been gone. *I guess I can throw all his paperwork in boxes and see if anyone needs them. Or I can label all the boxes and leave them outside of his accountant's office door. I'll put them all in the garage for now.*

"Laura?"

"I'm down the hall to the left" Laura yelled.

He practically ran down the hall. "Jennifer actually agreed to the arrangements. She was very understanding after I told her everything that had happened to you and even though she said she wasn't too keen on being away from Genevieve that long, we could always video chat at night."

"That is great. I will go ahead and book our tickets then. I wanted to make her room girly before she came here. Maybe I can ask Gloria to do it for me. I'll just give her a key and tell her what room."

"Laura, you don't have to do that. Aren't you planning on selling this house anyhow? What if the furniture doesn't go with the next house?"

"I am actually thinking of keeping it for when I have to work in New York. It's too hard to find anything and this is paid for and my mother-n-law is right down the road. This is a very nice and safe neighborhood. The schools are great. I would be a fool to sell it. Let me just call Gloria and see what she can do or we can go out tonight, pick some stuff out and have it delivered, I'll just make sure Gloria is here."

Joe shrugged his shoulders, "That is entirely up to you."

"Why don't you go relax and turn on the TV. I'll call Gloria while I book the airfare."

Laura called Gloria and told her what she was planning. "I will run over a credit card and the key and that way you are covered. It's my corporate card so you'll be fine. The bill comes to me anyway. Make it really cute for a three year old. Thank you so much."

She bounced into the living room and sat down next to Joe. "That is all set. Gloria is going to do the room for Genevieve."

"I just don't want you to spoil her."

"I'm not. I'm just setting up a room so it's appropriate for a little girl. All the rooms upstairs are set up for adults and are very boring for a child. Are you getting upset?"

"No. I know you want to make it special."

"Okay that's settled. Time to book the tickets. She opened her laptop and started looking. So, we'll stay at your house overnight and figure out what time would be most convenient to leave in the morning."

Laura looked over at Joe and he seemed to be in deep thought. "Is everything alright?"

"Yeah, I just don't know how this is all going to work with you bouncing back and forth from California to New York. How are we going to have a future if your heart is in New York? Your family is in New York. Your friends are in New York. Your life is in New York. It won't work."

"Joe, we haven't even started and you are already throwing in the towel? I'm losing you.

I told you I would follow you to California because that's where you have to be. Now, let's book these tickets and go from there. Don't freak out on me yet."

She hugged him, "Relax. Everything is going to be fine. I've booked our flight. Now we can either watch a movie or head upstairs or both."

The next morning they just packed a few things and she made sure she grabbed her spare key and had her corporate card and they headed over to Adam and Gloria's house.

"Thanks so much for doing this Gloria. I know you'll do an awesome job. It was so last minute."

"This will be fun for me because it's not my money." And she laughed.

"Okay, so we'll see you Monday evening. We figured we'd stay the long weekend that way Jennifer could spend it with Genevieve before she leaves and we can look at houses."

CHAPTER NINETEEN

Once they got out there, they grabbed a cab back to his house. "Ahh, home and my truck."

They grabbed their bags out of the taxi and walked into the house. Laura looked at him, "do you feel like looking at houses tomorrow?"

"We'll have Genevieve tomorrow."

"That's okay. It's even better when you have a kids view on things."

"I'm going to pick her up at seven tomorrow morning from Jen's."

Laura thought about Adam's beach house, "I wonder if I should check on the beach house. They said they were having professionals come in to clean it."

He looked at her, "That's your call. I still think it's pretty shitty that he was killed to make it look like a suicide."

"In my heart, I knew he wouldn't do something like that. It didn't seem like something he would do no matter how bad things got. That wasn't his style."

Joe wanted to change the subject, "Okay, we need some food in this house but not too much. Let's do a little grocery shopping. And just so I know what I'm doing. I either need to go back to work so I can pay my mortgage and bills or something has to happen here."

Laura said, "Oh yeah.....I'm going to write you out a check so that it will cover everything for a while until we figure out what we're doing. Is that okay?"

Joe's pride was starting to slide to an all-time low. "Laura, I appreciate what you are doing for me and Genevieve but I would rather work for a living to support myself. There is no worse feeling than having someone handing me money for nothing. You know. You still work even though you have plenty of money to retire with."

"I'm sorry. I'm not trying to make you feel that way at all. If you want to go back to work, that's fine. But not until you go to New York with me. When you come back you can. Just tell your work to read the papers or listen to the news and you are stuck in New York going through all the questioning and you're being held as a witness."

He looked at her, "You really think work will buy that?" And he grabbed her and took her to the bedroom.

He pulled her dress up over her head and threw it to the floor exposing her beautiful full breasts that he loved so much. He undid her bra and it fell to the floor as he teased her nipples. She unbuttoned his shirt and felt his rock hard chest and moved down to his jeans. He was already laying her down on the bed pulling off her lace panties. He took his pants off and started licking her nipples and working his way down to her belly button and he kept going until he found her warm wet spot ready for him but he wanted to play. He wanted to tease. He wanted to make her beg. She moaned and cried out but he kept going until she climaxed and screamed out and he was ready for her. He wanted her so bad. He slid it in and it took everything he had to keep from taking too much too soon. He just wanted to devour her. Her body drove him wild. He grabbed her breasts and played with her nipples. He started into her, faster and deeper and deeper and faster and she was crying out from pain and pleasure and he couldn't stand it anymore he yelled out as he came inside her.

He laid next to her in bed. "Your body drives me crazy. I just want you to know that."

Laura smiled, "Well, that's a good thing, right?"

"Yeah, if you never want me to leave you alone."

Laura got up and grabbed her stuff and walked into the bathroom. When she came out Joe was dressed and ready to go. "Now we can go to the store." And he gave her a kiss.

When they came back, they made a very late dinner and watched a little TV and both ended up falling asleep on the couch. Laura ended up waking both of them up from one of her nightmares at two O'clock in the morning so they both staggered into the bedroom disrobed to their undergarments and fell into bed.

Laura woke up around six thirty, and felt Joe up against her. She turned to face him, "What time do you have to leave here to get Genevieve?"

He said tiredly, "around six forty five. What time is it?"

"It's six thirty."

He started kissing her, "Well, I guess I have fifteen minutes to spare and he was already in her panties and whispered to her "take these off"

While she did that, he took his off and he pulled her on top of him and she started to ride him. He reached around and took off her bra and started fondling them which turned her on.

He saw that look in her eyes. It was power. And she was taking it. Harder and faster she went as she moaned. And then she cried out and he felt her tighten up but she kept going. She wanted more but it was too intense for him.........he couldn't hold off any longer, "I'm going to come." Laura started riding him faster and harder and she cried out I'm coming....I'm coming and as she came he finished with her.

"She looked down at him and smiled, "You need to get going."

"Well, you have to get off of me first."

She giggled, "Make me."

And he flipped her over and kissed her.

He headed to the bathroom with some clean clothes and emerged five minutes later, "Okay, I will see you in about a half hour."

"Okay, I'll have coffee on."

She laid there for a few minutes just thinking about his body. *God he has a beautiful body.* She thought. Just thinking about running her hands up and down his triceps and seeing his abs and shoulder muscles when he was on top of her got her all fired up.

She didn't feel like taking a shower before coffee so she threw on pajamas that she should have worn last night. And walked out to the kitchen. She waited for the coffee and walked onto the deck and sat for a minute enjoying the quiet.

And a chill went down her spine and made every hair stand up. *That was weird*, she thought because it was a warm morning. And then she thought she heard her name being called. It sounded like Kevin calling her name. *What the hell is going on?* And she sat there and waited. She thought maybe it was the breeze. And she felt the chill down her spine again and something told her she needed to call Adam to tell him that he needed to make sure Kevin's financial stuff was in order. All of a sudden a huge branch broke right in front of her. "Whoa" and she walked back into the house and grabbed the phone and called Adam.

"Gloria, you would probably believe me more than Adam. I am telling you the God's honest truth. I walked outside this morning and I got this chill down my spine and all my hair stood on end and then I heard someone calling my name and I listened again. It sounded like Kevin so I waited and I heard it again and I actually got that chill again and something told me to call you guys to tell you to check on Kevin's financial situation because he doesn't have anyone left. I think he was trying to say that there is unfinished business with you and Adam."

"What? That couldn't be but I'll let Adam know."

Laura was firm, "Look, You and Adam need to look into this. Kevin didn't have anyone else so maybe he left money to the kids or restaurants to you or the beach house to you or I don't know. You need to look at that. Tell Adam to look into that today. He has the people and the contacts. Tell him because Laura said so. Thanks Bye."

"Phew" She walked over and grabbed a cup of coffee just as she heard the truck pull in.

They walked in, "Hi Genevieve, Do I get a hug from you?"

Genevieve looked at Laura, "I get to go on a plane."

Laura said, "I know, this is your first time huh? It's going to be fun because we'll be in first class. AND you'll get to see where I live."

Joe pulled out some cereal and poured her a bowl. "Take a seat and have a healthy bowl of cheerios." He joked, "You want some coffee with that?"

Genevieve just said, "Yuck"

Laura agreed, "Yeah, it is pretty yucky, I don't know why adults drink it."

Laura looked over at Joe and said, "Oh, you have some more fire wood out back that you need to chop up."

He took a look. "What the heck happened?"

"It just happened while you were gone and I swear I heard Kevin calling my name."

"Excuse me?"

"I went outside while I waited for the coffee and I felt a chill through my body and every hair stood on end and then I heard someone call my name. I listened again and it sounded like Kevin calling my name. I don't know."

Joe looked at her in disbelief, "So, did you figure out what he wanted? Don't tell me………he still wants you."

"Stop" And she gave him the stink eye. "I'm thinking he has financial things that need to be dealt with. He has no family. Who would he leave his house to? Or what about his restaurants? I'm just thinking. Who knows?"

He looked at her strangely, "Well okay. I'm glad you were able to get it all straightened out."

"I know how it sounds. I was a little weirded out too you know."

"Anyways, do you have houses picked out that you want me and Genevieve to look at?"

Laura opened her laptop and pulled them up for a quick preview. "Let's stop at your bank so you can deposit that check to make sure bills are paid first." She pulled out her check book and wrote out the check and left it on the table.

Joe went to sit down by Genevieve and saw the check written out for two hundred thousand dollars. "Don't you think that check is a little much?"

"Joe, you have done a lot for me. Just don't say anything. Deposit it and you have it."

As they looked at the houses they narrowed it down to a couple. Well, Laura chose the two she liked as they were too overwhelming to Joe. He had never seen anything so big or elaborate with the marble floors and the winding staircases. But Genevieve seemed to like them. They were having fun watching her curiously run through the rooms.

They took her out for lunch and the day was so long she ended up falling asleep on the ride back.

"Does she have everything she came with?" Laura asked.

"No, she brought her backpack with her blankets and stuffed animal and doll that you bought her."

That made Laura feel good. "Do you want me to quietly run in and grab it then?"

Joe nodded, "Sure"

So, she grabbed her bag trying not to wake her and they took her back to her mom's.

Laura was finally able to meet Jennifer. She wanted Jennifer to feel more at ease with who she was handing her daughter over to for two weeks.

Laura said to her "Thank you so much for letting her stay for two weeks. I know it's a long time away, but I promise that she'll be well taken care of."

Jennifer asked Laura if she could watch Genevieve for a minute while she spoke to Joe in private. "Sure I can."

Laura was nervous. She thought for sure Jennifer was giving Joe a hard time right now. *What if she doesn't like me? She might think I'm trying to take her place. Oh God. This might not have a happy ending.*

She waited patiently while she played with Genevieve. And Joe and Jennifer came back in, Joe had a worried look on his face. He picked Genevieve up and gave her a hug and a kiss and told her he would be coming to get her on Sunday.

Jennifer surprised Laura and gave her a hug, "It was really nice meeting you."

Laura felt so guilty for having those thoughts, "It was really nice meeting you Jennifer. We'll see you on Sunday."

Once they got into Joe's truck, he was silent. Laura looked at him. "What's wrong? Doesn't she want Genevieve to go to New York?"

He shook his head, "It's not that. She was diagnosed with stage four ovarian cancer. She just found out today."

Laura sat back. She didn't know what to say. That was so unexpected.

She asked, "Is there anything I can do?"

"No, she'll be seeing a team of gynecologic oncologists this coming week to come up with a treatment plan."

"I'm so sorry Joe."

He pulled the truck over. "I don't think now is a good time for Genevieve and I to fly back to New York with you. Jennifer needs us here with her now."

Laura grabbed his hand, "And I totally understand that. I will just cancel and move flights around and do what I have to do so you can do what you have to do. Or do you want me to stay to help out?"

"No. I think it would be better if you went back to New York. I don't know what to expect or what the doctors are going to say."

She was disappointed inside but she really felt bad for what Jennifer was going through.

Once they got back to the house, she flipped open her laptop and did what she needed to do to rearrange flights. "I will take off tomorrow morning then so you can concentrate on Jen and Genevieve. They are priority right now."

He came over and hugged her. "I'm so glad you are understanding about all this. This was like a punch to the gut today. Totally unexpected."

Laura sounded confident, "I'm sure she'll be fine and if you guys need anything at all, I'm just a call and a flight away. You know I'll be out here in a moment's notice right?"

"Yes", he said almost in a daze. "I'm going to take a walk and get some fresh air.

She grabbed his hand, "You go take a walk. Take as much time as you need. I will fix dinner. Okay?"

And he walked out the door.

Dinner sat on the table with no Joe. She didn't want to bother him but she went outside to look for him and he was sitting in his truck. She walked over. "Dinner is done. You okay?"

"Yeah……….Just thinking. I'm coming in." and they walked in together.

It was a distant night. He took her to the airport the next morning and she assured him it was going to be okay and she would come back if he needed her. Again, he kept his distance from her and wasn't at all concerned about when he might see her again or calling him when she gets in so he knows she's safe. Nothing like that. It really started eating at her. She didn't want to make too much of it because of the circumstances but it really hurt.

CHAPTER TWENTY

When she got her cab home, she came in to a cheerful environment. Balloons and some stuffed animals and lots of fun stuff meant for Genevieve. There was a note on the kitchen island from Gloria. *"I hope you like what I picked out for the bedroom. I had so much fun. I might have went over budget. ☺"*

Laura smiled and decided to take a look upstairs. She walked into the bedroom and it was amazing. She gasped, *"This is unbelievable. I wish Genevieve was here right now."* She wanted to call Joe to tell him but she figured that wouldn't be fair. The bed was a four poster bed with pink sheer draped over and she had picked out the most beautiful bedding and draperies. Gloria went all out. *"Geez, I wonder how much this cost me?"*

Laura decided to go check on Mrs. Jennings. She thought she'd take a bottle of wine over with her. She and Joe had stopped over quickly the morning they left to leave Mrs. Jennings car and grab a cab from there but it was only but five minutes they were there and they were off. She decided it was a brisk but sunny day so she would walk over.

Mrs. Jennings was so happy Laura was there. She asked, "Where is the little one and Joe?"

"Well, there was some bad news so Joe and Genevieve couldn't make it here. Her mother found out she has cancer."

"Oh" Mrs. Jennings said. "How awful for that little girl."

Laura looked around, "Well, this house sparkles. Looks great."

"I didn't need a cleaning service. I can get around just fine. I'm not that old dear. I don't even have grandchildren yet. I'm only sixty six and they were treating me as if I was on my death bed. Good Lord."

Laura looked at her and handed her the wine. "Well, are you up for a glass or two of this?"

"Absolutely."

So they shared a couple glasses of wine and Laura wanted to know more about the family when the boys were little.

Mrs. Jennings told her, "We were like a regular family when they were small. Charles and I were both very involved in the boy's lives until Charles started becoming more well-known and sought after. Everyone wanted him to manage their investments so he started working late and going to dinner meetings and so on and so forth. That was around when the boys were ten and then it was like they didn't have a father at all. And I didn't have a husband."

"That's too bad. Kids need their father around. And I know what it's like to come home to no husband. But we're not going to talk about Edward."

Laura asked Mrs. Jennings, "Would it be okay if I could borrow your car tomorrow so I can go car shopping?"

"Yes. I don't need it for anything. You can take it."

"Thank you. It's a little inconvenient after my car was blown to pieces to get around without a car."

So they chatted for a while longer and Laura walked herself home.

As she looked around, she decided that the house just needed some re-decorating. After seeing the room redone for Genevieve, she thought maybe that's all this house needed was some major changes.

After she went car shopping and finally after two hours of haggling with the salesman, which she hated more than anything, she bought the same car she had and ended up going shopping to look for some new stuff for the house.

She had never done this because Edward never wanted to change anything. So, she went a little crazy and by the time she was done the Bentley was packed full.

She came home unloaded everything and started to put things into place. The master bedroom was the big one. She changed the look of everything in there to meet her style and it made a huge difference. She was actually starting to feel comfortable in this house. She thought to herself, *this is starting to look like MY house.*

She was back into her old routine, working all day and coming home to an empty house. Joe hadn't called so she figured she would leave them be. He would call when the time was right. She was definitely hurt though. And she missed him terribly. But she did hope Jennifer would be okay.

She finally got a call from her attorney Jack Larson to come to his office to sign paperwork and if she could bring Mrs. Jennings with her.

So, they both went in and sat down, Mrs. Jennings wondering why she was called in.

Jack started explaining to Laura. "Here is your paperwork for your alimony. Before I give it to you, I just want you to understand that it is not exactly what you thought you'd get but we are still looking at some of his other accounts and investments that are tied up."

She sighed, "Yeah, that figures. I don't care. Let's just get this done and over with."

She looked at it. "Is this amount correct? This is way more than what we had previously talked about." The paperwork she was looking at read she was entitled to two hundred thirty million dollars.

Jack nodded and smiled. "Yes, he still has investments that are held up and bank accounts overseas that we are still trying to track down but this is what we got you right now. He's good at hiding it. But this is what is owed to you due to the circumstances that have been presented."

And Laura shakily signed it not believing this was actually happening.

"You know what Jack? I actually feel that this money would benefit a lot of places that need it more than I. I want to donate thirty million dollars of this money to a couple of different places. One to children's cancer research and one to ovarian cancer research fund. Just split it 50/50."

Jack looked at her, "Are you sure you want to do that? That is a lot of money Laura."

"I am sure. This money has done nothing but bring greed and betrayal within the family and I'm going to turn that around and do something positive with it for once. I'm sure it has never seen a donation in its life. I might even decide to donate more. Or I might open up my own foundation. Yeah. That sounds like a great idea."

"Well, okay. I will do that for you. I will just change the paperwork here while you're in the office showing that you are donating thirty million dollars to the charities that you mentioned and the amounts each. So that will leave you with two hundred million dollars.

And he handed Mrs. Jennings paperwork. "Mrs. Jennings, because he confessed to admitting you to that hospital fraudulently and paying off the nurses to keep quiet and a whole list of other things, this is what is owed to you for pain and suffering."

Mrs. Jennings looked at the paperwork, she was entitled to thirty million dollars.

She signed the paperwork and gave them all her information and that was that.

Laura actually hugged Jack. "Thank you so much for everything you have done for me."

He said jokingly, "Don't think it didn't come with a price."

Laura said, "I'm sure it did. But you deserve it."

And they left, bank accounts feeling full.

"Mrs., Jennings?" And then Laura was interrupted.

"Call me Elizabeth."

Laura looked at her. "Okay. Elizabeth, would you mind dropping me off at the office first?"

"Not a problem. I think I'm going shopping anyhow and she laughed."

When Laura got to the office, she spoke to Adam and went back to work. Joe was still on her mind and then she thought of Kevin again and walked back into Adam's office.

"Did you start digging into Kevin's financial stuff?"

"Yes. And that is a mess. Still working on it. Trying to get some answers. I guess he left his beach house to us but he took a loan out against it for one of the restaurants so no one is paying on it. I should just let it go. Although its prime beach front property. I don't know."

Laura looked at him. "Okay. Just checking."

She walked back to her office thinking about it. *I could buy that house but after that whole ordeal, would I be able to walk back in there?*

It had almost been a week and she hadn't heard from Joe. *Maybe I'll just call him this weekend. I could go visit my parents this weekend too since I have nothing to do.*

She finished up her Friday, decided to grab some food on the way home in her brand new car and try and give Joe a call.

She got home and poured herself a glass of merlot and pushed dial. She didn't know what to expect. She got his voice mail. *Do I leave a message or do I just hang up?* She just decided to hang up.

CHAPTER TWENTY ONE

A month and a half went by and she went on with her life, visiting her family and reconnecting with her friends which was refreshing. She had cried herself to sleep some nights just figuring Joe was probably reconciling with Jennifer because of her condition. But she had a life too and once things settled and she realized she almost changed her life around and moved to California, she knew that was not what she wanted at all. But every time she had to walk upstairs, she would see that beautiful little room and it broke her heart.

Her friend Claire had called Laura and asked her if she wanted to go out to dinner with her and her husband and a "friend". Laura decided she would go. What would it hurt? It wasn't a date or anything.

Laura got to catch up with Claire. She hadn't seen her in such a long time. The "friend" was not that appealing to Laura. Nothing compared to Joe.

Claire didn't know Joe was back in the picture so the rest of the night, the girls pretty much sat and talked by the bar.

Laura looked back at the table, "I feel like we are being super rude."

Claire still pushing for more information said, "No. They're fine over there. They'll get over it. Now tell me more of what happened. How old was Kevin?"

So, Laura told her the entire story of what happened to her. And Claire could not believe it. Laura still had to hold back tears talking about Kevin. He will still have a special place in her heart. Always will.

When Laura mentioned something about moving to California, Claire reacted the same way her mom did.

"Laura, you can't possibly leave your entire life behind to go chase a guy from eight years ago. What about your whole identity? Your friends? Your family? You awesome job? You better think it through thoroughly before making that decision. That is not just a few towns over or even a state away. Just think about it. I'm only telling you this because I love you and care about you."

Laura hugged her, "I know. My mom said the same thing. It doesn't matter right now anyways. I haven't heard from him in over a month. His wife found out she has stage four ovarian cancer so I'm thinking maybe he reconciled with her to be with her and help her. I don't know. Maybe for Genevieve's sake. It's fine. I've come to terms with it and have started to move on."

Claire looked at her in the eyes, "Have you? You need to get out more Laura. All you do is work. That is not living life. I haven't seen you in months. If you need someone to talk to, you know I'm always there for you..........right?"

"Yeah. But I've been a little busy lately dodging death."

Claire gave her the stink eye, "I mean when you were dealing with all this with Edward. Months ago. Make sure you call me so that you at least get out once a week. I promise I won't try and fix you up UNLESS you ask me to."

Laura giggled, "It's a deal"

She spent a quiet Thanksgiving with Elizabeth Jennings and they had a wonderful day together. Laura usually would go to her parents for Thanksgiving but she knew her mother-n-law would be all alone.

"Mom Mrs. Jennings is going to be all alone for Thanksgiving and you are going to have a whole house full. I would feel better knowing that some family is here to spend Thanksgiving with her. Don't you think that's the right thing to do?"

Her mom sighed, "Yes, you're right. That's her first Thanksgiving out of that horrible place in a few years. We'll all miss you being here."

"I know but maybe next year, everyone can come out here for Thanksgiving for once. My house is so big I have a room for everyone. You know that. It would be fun. That way Mrs. Jennings can be involved. She would LOVE it."

Her mom got excited, "So, that means you're not moving to California?"

"I guess not. I haven't heard from Joe in a month and a half. Maybe he reconciled with Jennifer."

"Well, I know you don't want to hear it but sometimes things like this bring people back together. I'm really sorry Laura. It seems really unfair but just think of the one actually going through the cancer. THAT's unfair."

"I know mom. I do feel bad. I donated fifteen million dollars to ovarian cancer research. Maybe I should donate more. That just doesn't seem like enough. I'm thinking of starting my own foundation."

"Laura, that's a lot of money. I don't know what you got from Edward and I don't want to know because it's none of my business but you do what's in your heart and a foundation would be great if that's what you want to do. I love you, you know."

"I love you too. Tell dad the same. And have a Happy Thanksgiving."

Elizabeth made a great Thanksgiving feast just for the two of them and had a blast doing it. Laura went over there early so that she could help Elizabeth bake the goodies. Laura never gets the "good" cooking unless she goes home. They had a good old time laughing and Laura loved listening to Elizabeth with her stories. She just felt so bad that she no longer had any family to spend time with. But even if she did, would she want to spend time with them? They were so cold and evil. Laura was just glad that she was around to keep her company once in a while and that wouldn't happen if she moved to California so she guessed it was better that Joe was no longer in the picture.

Laura helped her clean up and Elizabeth insisted she take some food home with her when they heard a knock at the door and Laura got nervous almost ready to tell Elizabeth not to open it.   Elizabeth said, "I wonder who that could be." And walked over to answer it.

And Laura heard a familiar voice and immediately chills went down her spine. She looked over with tears in her eyes. She walked over and gave Joe the biggest hug. "Why are you here? What happened? Why haven't you called?"

Joe had tears in his eyes, "Jen didn't make it. They were too late. She had stage four and it had spread too quickly and there was nothing they could do for her."

"I'm so sorry Joe."

And she saw sad little Genevieve and picked her up, "mommy is in heaven with the angels. I won't see her anymore but she can see me." And she had the saddest face Laura had ever seen.

Laura put her down and knelt in front of her. "Yes, your mommy is in heaven and that's the best place to be."

Elizabeth was standing there taking this all in and she had tears in her eyes hearing little Genevieve talk about her mom with the angels. She has never had this kind of love in this house ever. "All of you, come in here and warm up. There is so much Thanksgiving dinner left. You are going to eat."

Then Elizabeth looked at little Genevieve with her teary eyes and said, "Come here sweetheart, I have something special for you. Do you like pie?"

Genevieve smiled, "yummy."

Elizabeth gave her a small sliver of everything so she could try them all. She was loving it and thought it was great having the dessert before dinner.

Joe looked at Elizabeth and said, "Thank you so much for the dinner and being so welcoming."

She smiled, this is what I've been waiting for. I haven't had love in this house for a long, long time. Not since Laura has walked into my life and she grabbed Laura's hand.

They all sat down and enjoyed each other's company. Elizabeth with her wise words of comfort helped ease the pain of the loss and she was enjoying every minute of Genevieve. "I will make sure there are lots of toys for this little one next time she is here. You are staying in New York?"

And then there was silence.

Laura looked at Joe waiting for a response.

He looked at Genevieve and then looked at Laura, "I guess there is nothing holding me back now. And since you have family here, and he looked at Elizabeth, maybe it would be best."

Elizabeth smiled and said, "Oh good. Now I have a little one to spoil."

And Laura stood up in front of Joe and said, "I have one more thing to tell you."

"What is it?"

Laura whispered in Joe's ear, "We're having a baby."

Joe looking in total surprise and looked at Elizabeth before responding, "But I thought.........you know."

Laura shrugged her shoulders and said, "Some things are miracles."

Joe picked Laura up and gave her the biggest hug. "This is awesome. We're having a baby."

Elizabeth clapped her hands together, "Well isn't this going to be a Thanksgiving to remember."

Don't miss Paradise Valley, Lost and Found.

Coming in Winter 2015/16 –

Dangerous Game of Deception

(Book 2 of the series)

www.jodivillone.com

And you can follow me on twitter

www.ingramcontent.com/pod-product-compliance
Lightning Source LLC
Chambersburg PA
CBHW070853180626
46817CB00003B/763